The SINNER in he

STACY RUSH

THE SINNER IN ME

Cover Design by Stacy Rush
Formatting by Stacy Rush

ISBNs:
Paperback ISBN: 9798992765656

AUTHOR'S NOTE

If you're new to my work, welcome—and consider this your warning. I write dark, intense stories that aren't for the faint of heart. This story, even though it's short—is anything but sweet.

The Sinner in Me is an *erotic* romance. Which means the sexual content is high, but it does have a plot. Although this is a work of fiction, there is a lesson to be had in the end. For those familiar with the dynamics in this book, you will be well aware of the possible consequences that may occur. You must have an open mind to truly understand and enjoy this read.

I write unapologetically dark fiction, often laced with graphic sexual content and extreme themes—perhaps a sprinkle of taboo, too. I know this isn't for everyone, and that's okay. If this kind of storytelling isn't for you, I ask that you prioritize your mental health and choose something gentler. No hard feelings.

But if you're ready to embrace the darkness—I promise you, you'll love the ride.

THE SINNER IN ME

STACY RUSH

DISCLAIMER

No part of this book may be reproduced or transmitted in any form or by any means, electronic or mechanical, including photocopying, recording, or by any information storage and retrieval system without the written permission of the author.

This is a work of fiction. Unless otherwise stated, all names, characters, businesses, places, events, and incidents in this book are either the product of the author's imagination or used in a fictitious manner. Any resemblance to actual persons, living or dead, or actual events is purely coincidental.

Please do not try any of the sexual practices found in this book without the guidance of an experienced professional. The author is not responsible for any harm, loss, injury, and/or death resulting from the use of the information in this.

TRIGGER WARNING

Although this is a short novella, just like my other books, it contains dark themes and mature content. If you are sensitive to stories containing BDSM, Forced Proximity, Objectophilia, Dub/Con, Non-Dub/Con, Dom/sub, Captivity, Murder, Humiliation, Suicide, Nudity, Violence, Revenge, and other possible triggers. Please be sure to read thoroughly because your mental health matters... Find the FULL MENU on my website at authorstacyrush.com

v

DEDICATION

For those of you who are expecting a love story—this is not it. It's a warning for those who like to play with fire. Even the experienced ones can get burned when an obsession becomes ruinous...

PROLOGUE

Ayla

The club is packed tonight, but it doesn't stop me from forcing my way through the crowd to where I know *he* is going to be. I've watched him every night this week, and tonight, I want to be part of his brutality.

Not many women can handle him, and those who do take a chance with the Beast either run out of the room crying or walk cockeyed. I've seen the things the Beast does to the women who enter his chamber, and I must say, I've never been so turned on in my entire twenty-three years.

Is it wrong of me to want someone so badly that I'm willing to do anything to be with them? Have I mentioned that I've also never seen the Beast's face? He wears a mask all night long—a mask of a beast—yet something about him calls out to me.

The guy stands at least six feet five inches, which is taller than my five feet four inches, and he's built like a house. Solid muscle makes up the exterior of the Beast, and he's very well endowed.

I spot him walking down the hall toward his chamber. A petite woman walks beside him in a thong and corset. Her hair is bright red, and when she turns, her lipstick is just as bright. She smiles up at the masked beast as he swings his chamber door open and allows her to enter first.

Just before he enters the room, he turns my way, and I swear our eyes meet. However, I can't be entirely sure that he looks at me. I'm not close enough, and the dim lighting doesn't allow me to see his eyes through the mask, but I swear I feel the weight of his stare.

Hurrying to the viewing window, I come to a stop just at the edge of the crowd. Beast's performances are well-known and very popular among the voyeurs. He goes hard and has no mercy. Those who can't handle it and say their safe word get booted out immediately, and the Beast goes in search of another victim.

I want to be that victim tonight.

"What do you suppose he will do tonight?" a woman beside me asks the man she's hanging all over.

There's amusement in her tone as if she's counting on the Beast to do something unruly, which can be the case some nights. The man fondles her breasts as he nibbles on her neck, but pauses to respond to her question.

"Does it look like I give a fuck? I only bring you here because your cunt drips every time you watch the Beast, and I need you nice and wet."

The woman giggles, finding his crude answer funny. I then fade the couple out and give all my attention to the man behind the mask.

The Beast forces the redhead to her knees, and she drops down onto her hands, but then, another door opens, and in walks a beautiful blonde. The woman, on her hands and knees, tries to get up, but a single word from the Beast causes her to resume her position on all fours.

My pulse begins to really race at this turn of events. I haven't seen him with two women at the same time since I came to this club; this is all new. Licking my lips, my attention never wavers from the room.

Beast points to the redhead, and the newcomer strips off her robe and sits on the redhead's lower back as if she's a chair. The blonde then leans back and spreads her legs. I watch in fascination as the Beast steps up between her legs, making the redhead widen her legs also, and then he kneels.

This makes him the perfect height as he grabs the blonde's hips and thrusts his length into her. He proceeds to fuck the blonde as the redhead is used as a piece of furniture.

"Come for me," Beast orders and flicks the woman's clit with his finger.

She winces, but me? I can feel the phantom pain of the flick as if it's being done to me, and I crave more of it. An intense throbbing erupts between my legs, and I squeeze my thighs together to try and subdue the ache.

The blonde cries out more and more as he flicks and then slaps her clit. Suddenly, the woman moans, and the Beast pulls out and squirts all over the redhead.

I've never seen anything like it, and not realizing I'm doing it, I brace myself against the window with one hand as my other hand slips up my skirt and rubs my clit until I'm coming right there in front of everyone.

"Oh my! Someone enjoyed the show." The woman beside me is gleaming in my direction as I come down from the orgasm.

Oh shit!

My head snaps to the window, and a dark pair of eyes bore into mine from the other side. The Beast is standing just on the other side, staring at me. His fists are balled up at his sides, and his chest heaves up and down.

My eyes lower to where his cock still hangs out, but it pulses as cum drips from the tip. I don't know what's happening. Did I miss something? Is the Beast mad that I interrupted the scene?

Instead of staying to find out, I turn and hurry from the voyeur hallway and then the club, not daring to look back.

Beast POV

She's fucking perfect. I knew she would be. I've been following her around ever since I first saw her online. I had to find out more about her, so I did what I do best: I searched for her online and offline. I know everything there is to know about the little imp, and soon, I will have her.

I watch as she gets into her car, and then I get on my bike. Something spooked her from the club tonight, but I won't let that stop me. It was nothing to get her to start coming here. I knew her interests were on the darker side, so all it took to get my little imp here was to ensure she found the card I left for her.

The small, black business card I had left on the front seat of her car was all it took. Two days later, she was at *The Lair*.

Following my imp home, I park outside in the alley beside her building. I'll watch until her lights go off and she's tucked in for the night; it's what I typically do. However, a few minutes later, my little imp steps back outside, carrying a garbage bag, and places it at the curb.

I watch as a man approaches her.

3

"Aren't you a pretty little thing. Want some company?" he asks, making my blood boil.

"In your fucking dreams," my imp replies, screwing up her face.

I grin.

"How about I teach you a lesson in respect?" the man sneers.

"How about you walk away and leave me the fuck alone?" my girl retorts and tries to walk past him, but his arm snakes out and spins her around.

I'm just about to intercede when my little imp brings her knee up and gets the man right in his junk. The asshole immediately grabs himself, cursing, while my girl hurries back into her apartment.

Ensuring she's inside, I stalk toward the fucker who dared put his hands on my girl, and I wrap my arm around his neck, putting him in a chokehold. His hands come up, gripping my arm as he kicks out. I pull him back into the alley with me, out of sight from any prying eyes.

"You dared touch what is mine!" Spittle flies from my clenched teeth as I ask, spraying the inside of my helmet.

That asshole tries saying something, but can't. The hold I have on him is too tight. Letting him go, I shove his head into the brick wall as I pull out my tactical knife.

"Please! I'm sorry... I didn't know!"

"No, you're not, but you're about to be..."

Gripping his hair, I slam the fucker's face into the wall one, two, three times before plunging my knife into his left eye. Covering the scream coming from his mouth with my hand, I yank my blade out and stab his other eye.

"This is for even looking at my girl. And this,"—I pull it back out only to embed it in the *head* that was doing all the thinking—"Is for touching her, and thinking you were going to get some! That virgin pussy is all mine, and no piece of shit like yourself will ever touch what is mine!"

In the end, I bring the knife up, and in one swift motion, I slice it across his neck, ending his pathetic life. Swiping my blade against the fucker's jeans, I clean it off and place it back into its holder at my side. I glance up and see my little imp's lights are all off, so I hop back on my bike and head home.

ONE

Ayla

I've always known that something was wrong with me deep inside. I wasn't like other girls. When talking about boys, my friends would share stories of how their boyfriends had done something so sweet and treated them like delicate flowers. I'd scoff inwardly, calling those boys pansies. My mind always turned dark when I thought of the perfect guy for me. I don't see roses and jewelry—instead—I see hand necklaces and restraints.

Let me just say, I've never had intercourse because I've never met a guy I thought would pleasure me the way I crave. I've been on dates before, but they've always been sweet and treated me with utmost respect. I do appreciate them for that, but just once, I want someone to grip my throat, shove me against the wall, and *take* our first kiss.

Walking into the First Financial building for my first day of work. I try to clear my head of all these thoughts. Now isn't the time to be thinking about hand necklaces and being choked. I can't screw this up; my father helped me get this personal assistant job with his friend's company, and I wouldn't want to disappoint him.

I take the elevator up to the twenty-fourth floor and step out into a massive reception area. Swallowing hard as I look at my surroundings, I slowly walk up to the desk where an older woman with salt and pepper hair smiles up at me.

"Can I help you?"

"Uh, yes. I'm Ayla Kennedy. I'm—"

"Mr. Silverman's new assistant," she finishes warmly. "I'm Amilia, his receptionist, and let me just say how thrilled I am to get some help around here."

I relax instantly. The woman's welcoming smile calms my nerves. This is the most challenging aspect of getting a job. I have a college education, but when it comes to interviews, I fuck them up because I get nervous. I should be ashamed that I needed my father to get me a job, but I'm extremely grateful.

"Yes, I'm the new assistant." I return her smile.

"Well, let me show you Mr. Silverman's office before he arrives. I'll then show you around and get you settled in at your desk."

"Thank you. I'd appreciate it," I reply, not really knowing what else to say.

The tour is overwhelming, but I'm excited to get started. I want a job that will make my family proud, since everything else I do doesn't. I won't apologize for how I made my way through college. When your parents are strict and want you to be responsible while still trying to get an education, you sometimes have to think outside of the box.

"Miss Kennedy..."

"Sorry," I say quickly as I give Amilia my full attention once more. "It's just so..."

"A lot, I know." The older woman giggles. "You'll get used to it. Mr. Silverman isn't too demanding himself; it's just the work that's demanding."

A phone rings in the distance, and Amilia holds her finger up and presses the piece that I didn't notice she had in her ear.

"First Financial, Gunner Silverman's office. How may I help you?" There's a pause, and then Amilia smiles. "Yes, Sir. I'm with her now." Another long pause, and then she says, "Of course, Sir. I will show her everything and make sure it's on your desk by the end of the day. Good luck today."

When Amilia presses the earpiece a second time, she smiles at me. "Well, I guess it's only you and me today. Mr. Silverman has to travel out of town to sign a few contracts that came up last minute. He's asked me to show you the files that he will need this week, but he wants you to go over them and ensure everything is in order."

"Oh, okay. That shouldn't be a problem."

At least the pressure of meeting the boss has been removed. I've heard that he can be nice, but that he's very particular when it comes to his employees. He likes to run a smooth ship, but isn't that all businessmen?

Once Amilia leaves me to get to work, I immerse myself in numbers and the day flies by. I love numbers. I guess you can say I'm a nerd when it comes to them, but it's all I'm good at. By the time I leave the office, I'm tired and in need of a tall glass of wine.

Throwing my keys in the bowl on the table when I walk in the door, I kick off my heels, sighing. It's been a while since I wore heels for eight hours straight; I'd forgotten how much I despise them.

Going to the fridge, I pull out the bottle of red wine I bought, knowing I'd need it today, and I pour myself a full glass. I'm not one who smells my wine before guzzling a big gulp, and savoring the taste as it slides down my throat.

I make my way to the spare room, where all my equipment is set up, and I start turning on all the monitors and cameras. Once everything is up and running, I take a seat and log into my *Just For You* account to check on my last video.

Hm, one point three million views and three hundred twenty-six new subscribers—nice.

I've been doing cam work since my first year of college, after I got fired from my fourth job. I couldn't keep up with working and studying, so I did what I had to do and became a camgirl.

It only takes a few hours a week, and it pays my bills. I cut back after graduating since I no longer needed to pay tuition, but it's still more than I'd like to be doing.

I'm not saying I hate it, but when you're a virgin, getting yourself off on camera for thousands of subscribers, it becomes boring. I need more than my own hand and a dildo.

I need a nice girthy cock slamming into me, owning my pussy, and ensuring that I feel it for days after. Am I wrong for thinking this when I've never had a real one inside me? Maybe, but just the thought of it has me panting like a bitch in heat.

Opening my chest of toys, I decide on the *Double Header* for tonight's viewing, and then head to the closet to find the perfect outfit. I want to make this a good show because I'm not sure how much longer I'll be doing this, now that I have a real job, and I want to make it memorable for one particular viewer.

This viewer pays well, and they're very demanding as a result. However, they never ask me to do anything that I don't enjoy.

Fucking myself in front of the camera doesn't bother me. What does is that I have to make it look good because I never go in deep enough to break my hymen. I'm not really wanting to lose my virginity to a fucking dildo. However, if it happens, it happens.

It doesn't take long at all for my subscribers to tune in as soon as they receive the notification that I'm live. Most of them are small timers; those who only have enough to pay for me to finger myself or ask to see my breasts.

After about two hours, I'm getting ready to log off when a new message pops up. Excitement passes through when I see it's my big baller.

Bigdaddy_69: Let's play, CamBaby.
CamBaby: What will it be tonight, Big Daddy?

I'm glad I brought the double header out; it's Big Daddy's favorite.

Bigdaddy_69: You know what I like, CamBaby. Do you have it?

I hold up the dildo.

CamBaby: I always cum prepared for you, Big Daddy.
Bigdaddy_69: That's such a good girl. You know what I like, get that pussy all wet and take it fast and hard for me.

Grabbing the lube, I prepare myself for the show, making it as sexy as I can for him. I've already received notification of his five-thousand-dollar payment.

Turning the video camera on for him, I begin by inserting the double header into my ass because it's easier this way. By the time I inch it into my pussy, I'm already moaning in pleasure.

"Mm, that's it. You're my perfect butt slut, CamBaby. I want to meet you, so I can fill you up so full," Big Daddy states.

He always says this, but it never happens. I don't date my online clients.

With the head of the dildo only inside of my pussy a few inches, I bounce up and down, making it look like I'm taking it deep, just like he likes it.

"Oh, God, Big Daddy. I'm going to come for you!"

"That's my good little slut. Come for Daddy. Fuck that toy and come all over it."

I don't know what it is about this client, but I always feel the need to please him. Not just on video, but even through chat, he's got an aura that demands obedience, and I want to give him everything he wants.

With that being said, I push the dildo in even deeper, and gasp at the fullness and slight pain. I've just done what I said I never would—I broke my hymen. Looking down, I see the streaks of red on the rubber dick, and for some reason, it turns me on more.

Big Daddy must understand what just happened because he snickers, "Finally, CamBaby. I've been waiting for you to take it all. You're ready."

Not understanding what he means, I simply reply, "I'll always be ready for you, Big Daddy."

By the end of our video chat, I'm spent, and we say good night. I don't bother putting anything away right now; I'm too exhausted. I'll come in here tomorrow and clean everything up. Tonight, I need my bed and a good night's sleep.

two

Ayla

I finally get to meet my new boss a few days later. I'm already running late and have to rush to the elevator before the door closes.

"Hold the elevator, please!" I call out.

A large hand reaches out, stopping the doors from closing, and I hurry inside. My chest is heaving from running, and I'm breathing heavily.

"Thank you so much. This morning has already been hectic. I really didn't want to be late for work," I explain, even though it wasn't necessary.

"You're welcome."

Those are the only words that come out in a deep, baritone voice. My head snaps up. The dominance that the man's tone holds catches my attention immediately. However, when I get a look at the man, I practically lose all the air in my lungs.

He's fucking gorgeous!

Not everybody may feel the same way I do, but I love the imperfections that people have. I say this because this man, with his dark looks, Roman nose, and chiseled jaw line, has a long, puckered scar that runs from his left temple all the way down his cheek in a jagged line, ending in the middle of his neck.

The imperfection doesn't detract from his beauty, but instead, adds to it. At least in my eyes, it does. He's also much older than my twenty-three years—I'd say late thirties, possibly early forties, but *damn*.

His dark eyes fix on mine with intimidation. The submissive in me instantly looks down. I close my eyes as soon as his scent hits me. A musky sandalwood scent that screams *all man*. A throbbing begins between my legs, making me squeeze my thighs together.

The elevator ride seems to take forever. My heart thuds rapidly against my chest the whole ride up to the twentieth-fourth floor.

Shit, we're going to the same floor.

Just before the doors open, the man speaks once more. "It's so nice to finally meet you, Miss Kennedy. I'll take my coffee in my office."

My head snaps up once again when what he says registers. This is Mr. Silverman, my boss!

"Y-yes, Sir. I'll bring it right away."

He steps off the elevator first, not giving me a second thought, and I just stare after him.

Fuck my life...

After sitting in on two conference calls and running a handful of errands for Mr. Silverman, I'm relieved when he announces that he's leaving for the day. It's not that I don't like him. He's very intimidating, and it was disturbing that he refused to look at me when I was near, yet, as soon as I turned my back, I could swear I felt his eyes on me.

The rest of the afternoon went by like my first few days, and by the time I get home, I'm ready for a glass of wine. However, I'm still feeling the effects of meeting my new boss this morning and have decided to go back to The Lair.

It's been a while since I ran out of the club, and I'm feigning to go back. I'm sure the Beast has forgotten all about me. After all, he has plenty of women to entertain. Well, those that aren't afraid of him, that is.

Dressing in my black, pleated mini skirt that allows my butt cheeks to play peek-a-boo, I then pull on a dark purple mesh crop top. I decide to be brave and go braless, letting my taut nipples poke out and be on display. I then slip on my black combat boots and throw my hair up in pigtails.

Looking at myself in the full-length mirror, I remind myself of a brat, and I grin. Good. Maybe then I can find someone to give me a nice, long spanking. I need to feel that pain.

Adding some black liner and a slight blush, I call it good and head out. It's already dark out, so I don't have to worry about too many people seeing me in my state of dress. Not that I care if they do, as long as a little kid doesn't see me; that's just wrong.

I'm surprised to find the club packed for a weekday, but it doesn't take long to find out why. It's a special night. Once a month, the dominants get to pick the sub they want to scene with, and the sub has to accept. Of course, the submissive can choose to leave the club if they don't want to participate, but if they stay, they are consenting to scene with the Dom who chooses them.

Excitement fills me as I look over the club, picking out a few of the Doms whom I've seen in the past and wouldn't mind working with. I want to put myself in their path and hope one of them chooses me.

I'm only about halfway through the club when I feel a hand wrap around my bicep.

"You're with me tonight," a gruff voice states, and I turn to see a good-looking guy.

He's not one that I know, but I don't think I'll mind. Smiling, I nod and let him lead me back through the crowd. However, we don't make it too far before a growl erupts, and I'm pulled out of the dominants' grasp.

"She's *mine* tonight."

I'm pulled against a hard body, and the scent that wafts past my nose tells me exactly who it is. The look on the other guy's face confirms it as his eyes widen and he nods before turning and hurrying away.

There's only one guy in this club who puts that fear on the faces of others—the *Beast*.

The man towers over me, and when he bends over, shoving his face into the crook of my neck and inhales, I begin to tingle.

"Mm, you smell delicious, brat. I don't typically like brats, but this beast is craving a taste of you. You will be a good girl and come with me, won't you?" Beast pauses before adding, "Or are you going to run away like last time?"

Oh shit. He remembers!

"I'll come..."

"Oh, that you will—over and over again."

15

Fuck, just listening to him talk to me almost has me creaming my thong.

As if he can read my thoughts, Beast reaches down and shoves his hand between my thighs, feeling the wetness already pooling at my core.

His chuckle is anything but pleasant.

"Such a little slut for me already, huh? I don't think you need these anymore," Beast states and then rips my thong from my body.

The few people who witness the exchange chuckle and watch on in amusement. It doesn't bother me none. It turns me on to be watched, and being humiliated at the same time only adds to it. The only thing that will turn me on more than I am right now is if Beast were to bend me over and force me to take him in front of everyone. I'm fucked up, I know.

You may ask how a virgin can feel as I do, and my answer will always be the same—the fuck if I know. I may have broken my hymen, but I've never had a real cock inside me before, and I'm so ready for it to happen.

"Kneel, imp," Beast orders as soon as we enter the room he has chosen.

Glancing at my surroundings, I see that he has chosen the cave-like room, and it sends goose bumps across my skin. This is the room where he goes animalistic. It's his true habitat.

I drop to my knees before him, but I don't look down. If he's going to keep calling me an imp, then I'll act like one. I may be looking for trouble, but that's exactly what I need.

Gripping my cheeks, he squeezes and asks, "What's your safe word?"

Wanting to be the bratty imp that he thinks I am, I reply, "Fuck me."

Beast smirks and raises his brow.

"You want to play that game? We can go without the safe word, and you will take *everything* I give you."

"I'm not scared," I mumble through his grip on my face.

He scoffs.

"We'll see about that, imp."

He then spits in my mouth, and I savor the taste of his minty saliva. I want more—I need more, but I won't push it.

16

Beast moves to the corner of the room, where he pulls a contraption down from the wall. I'm familiar with it and excited that he's going to use it on me.

Coming to stand behind me, he drops to his knees and pulls my arms back, securing a cuff around each bicep. He then takes the third cuff and closes it around my neck, immobilizing me. Gripping my arms, he hauls me back to my feet just as the viewing window opens up to the crowd.

"Let's give them a good show, little imp. Shall we?" Reaching around, Beast tears my top right down the middle, exposing me to all.

I don't think about what I'm going to wear home. All I can think about is that I'm finally going to have Beast all to myself.

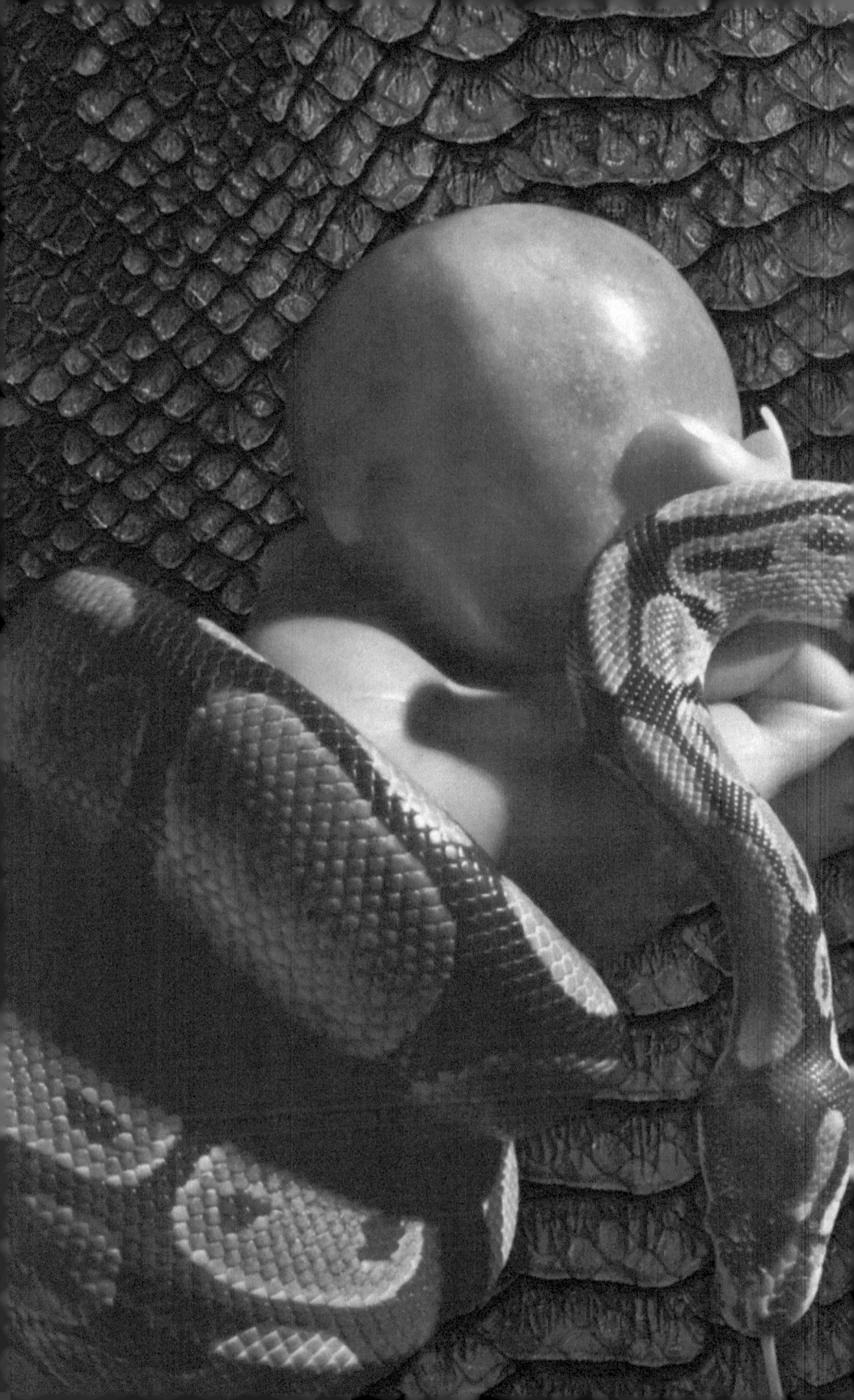

THREE

Beast

I had been watching Ayla for a while now. The first time she entered The Lair, I knew exactly who she was. After all, I had been the one to ensure she found out about the club. Now, I have her in my domain, and I have no plans on letting her go. Life as she knows it will no longer exist unless I say it does.

As I bare her beautiful breasts to the crowd, anger builds inside of me. Ayla is mine, and as much as I want to keep her all to myself, I want all to know that everything they see here is mine and is off limits.

My little imp doesn't realize what she's gotten herself into. Ayla is different from other women. She's got a darkness within her that I think may match my own with a bit of help. I've been searching for the perfect partner, and Ayla seems to fit the description.

I've put a lot of work into placing her in my path in her everyday life. My plan was to groom her until I knew she was ready, but the beast inside me doesn't want to let her walk out of here.

My beast gets whatever he wants.

It's why I've brought her to this room. Not many people have access to it, and only I have a say in when voyeurs may come this deep into the club and watch. This cave-like room will be Ayla's home for the foreseeable future, unless she proves herself worthy to be by my side immediately.

I move my little imp over to the harness that hangs from the ceiling and attach the hooks to her arm restraints. Then, I lift each of her legs and place them in the straps that keep her spread wide open for me.

This next part is going to be my favorite. It's where she's going to find out who I am exactly and just how involved I am in her life.

I walk to the chest of toys and open the lid, pulling out the item I need. It's the exact replica of another, and when I turn to show my little imp, her eyes widen.

"Look familiar?"

"N-no...it can't be."

"Ah, but I had to get one to keep here for when you arrived. After all, we both know it's our favorite toy to fuck that sweet cunt with, isn't it?"

"B-Big Daddy?"

"Yes, CamBaby?"

"How?"

"You don't worry about that. Just know that I'm going to take care of you," I croon as I caress her face.

"But I thought you were going to have sex with me?"

I tsk and shake my head.

"You haven't earned my cock yet, but you will. I'll make sure of it."

Lubing up the double-headed dildo, I stand behind my little pet so everyone can see as I work it into her tight little ass just like she does.

"Don't be afraid to moan for them, CamBaby. We both know you love your ass fucked."

"Please! What's going on? I don't understand..." she states before a moan drips from her lips as I begin thrusting the toy in and out.

"You don't need to understand yet. Just know that I'm going to take care of you from now on." I then lube the other end of the dildo and push it into her soaked pussy.

The only difference between hers and mine is that mine vibrates. I turn it on when I have both ends deep inside her and she screams, coming instantly.

"Beast, please!" Ayla pleads as her body jerks while she tries humping the toy in the air.

There's laughter from the crowd at the sight of her doing so, but I ignore them as I take one of her nipples into my mouth and bite down.

Another scream falls from her lips, and I chuckle before doing the same to the other. She likes it. My little imp is a pain slut.

I grip her hair and make her look me in the eyes. "Tell me you're mine," I snarl.

"I'm yours, Beast—I'm yours!"

"That's right. From here on out, you are mine!"

Lifting my arm, I slice my hand on a sharp stone jutting out of the ceiling and place it on her mouth.

"Drink it," I order.

Ayla surprises me and starts sucking on my hand, drinking my blood, and sealing her fate. Unfortunately, with her tied up the way she is, all I can do is sink my teeth into her breast, breaking the skin, and drinking from her as she cries out and comes.

Wiping my mouth when I'm done. I stare at her wide eyes and grin.

"It's done. We are one, and you are mine. Welcome home, little imp."

I allow her to sleep after our little show, and as she does, I leave to collect the few people from the crowd who dared laugh at my little imp earlier. Two men and a woman. They were a threesome, so it made it really easy to lure them back to my cave.

Locking us in this section of the club, the Dungeon Masters know better than to try and get in. This is my club, and if I want to do sketchy shit, I'm going to do it. I pay them well to turn a blind eye to my extracurricular activities.

When we walk into the room and I see my little imp still asleep, I grin. The leash that I've locked around the collar she now wears around her neck won't allow her to go too far. She looks perfect as she is—naked and all mine.

"Oh, do we get to play with your little pet, Beast?" the woman asks as she walks over to the bed and runs her hand up my imp's bare leg.

"Unless you want to lose that hand, I suggest you remove it from my property," I sneer.

The woman giggles, then says, "My bad. I thought—"

"You thought wrong. I brought you here for something else."

"Beast?" A drowsy voice floats over to me.

"Yes, little imp. I'm here."

"What's going on?" she asks.

"Well, I was waiting for you to wake up, so I can show you just how much you mean to me."

"What?" Ayla asks, confused.

I join her on the bed and take her hand. "I want you to know the lengths I will go to for you. Nobody will ever make fun of what is mine."

Ayla lifts her hand and feels the collar and leash. She automatically starts pulling on the collar, but it won't come off without the key.

I shove her hand away. "Don't injure yourself, or else I'll have to restrain your wrists."

"Beast. What is this?"

I get up and move to stand by one of the other men.

"They were laughing at you, little imp. When you were fucking the dildo, they found it funny when you were humping the air. Nobody laughs at you. Do you understand me?"

Before another word is spoken, I reach up and twist the guy's neck. A loud crack echoes through the room, and he drops like a bag of potatoes.

"What the fuck?" The other guy jumps back. "Y-you killed h-him! You killed Alex!"

I shrug.

"You really are a beast!" the guy states as he reaches for his screaming woman. "Come on, Tara. Let's—"

I rush them as they turn, twisting his neck mid-sentence. The woman runs to the door, continuing to scream, but she can't get out. I locked it as we came in.

"Beast?" A whisper of a voice comes from the woman still in the bed. "Tell me you didn't..."

"Kill them?" I finish when Ayla doesn't. "Yes, I did. Now you know the lengths I'll go to for you."

Ayla shakes her head.

"No. It's wrong..."

She says this, but she doesn't seem to be as upset at seeing me take a life as this other woman is. Rolling my eyes, I grab the woman by her hair, tired of her screaming, and thrust her onto the bed.

"Finish her. Prove to me that you're mine," I tell my little imp, but she shakes her head again.

"I may be fucked up, but I can't kill someone just for laughing at me, Beast."

I understand how she feels. I don't enjoy taking a life, but people leave me no choice sometimes. Since the woman is already on the bed, I press my hand to the back of her head and smother her face into the mattress.

The woman squirms and tries to get out of my grip, but it's no use. I stare at Ayla the entire time, watching her watch me take this woman's life. She doesn't look scared—more like fascinated, and that makes me hard.

My little imp may not like killing someone, but I do believe she gets aroused by me doing so. I'll have to remember that.

Once the woman is still, I let go and climb onto the bed beside her still form. Pulling my cock out, I reach for my little imp and pull her up so my cock is inches from her mouth.

"Open up, and take what I give you. Thank me for what I've done for you, imp."

Shaking her head, she's about to deny me, but I won't allow it. Instead, I take a different route.

"You know you want my cock, imp. Now take it before I change my mind and you don't get anything."

That does the trick. Forgetting that there's a dead woman beside us, Ayla lets me use her mouth to get myself off.

23

FOUR

Ayla

I should be petrified of the Beast or, at the very least, scared, but I'm not. Nobody has ever cared enough for me to actually kill someone. My parents love me, but would they ever kill someone for laughing at me?

I know, I must be fucked up in the head, but as I watched Beast smother the woman right beside me, then make me take him in my mouth, it turned me on like no other. Even though I've felt a darker side to myself, I've always been a good girl growing up. Perhaps that's why this isn't affecting me as it should.

What I am upset about is being chained up like a dog and not being allowed to leave. I'm sure my new boss has already sent out a termination letter since I've been a no-show for the past four days. The only positive part about my situation is that Beast has come in and gotten me off every day.

The lock on the door clicks, and in walks my beautiful captor. I haven't seen his face yet, but to me, he's the most beautiful soul I've ever met. Well, that's what my libido keeps telling me anyway.

Beast walks in, carrying a tray with what appears to be medical supplies on it. Furrowing my brow, I scrutinize his every move.

"I have a present for you, little imp," Beast states as he sets the tray on the stand by the bed.

"What is that?" I ask as I take in what looks like a needle-like device, a syringe, and a bandage. "What do you plan to do?" I try to back away, but he catches my ankle and yanks me back.

"I want to fuck you, and for me to do that, you need to be on birth control."

"Then take me to a doctor!" My voice rises a little, causing him to stop and glare at me.

"Don't take that tone with me, little imp."

"I-I'm sorry. I just don't understand why this is happening. I need to get back to my life..."

"Your life is with me now, and as soon as you realize that, then we can discuss your freedom." He takes my left arm and cuffs it to the headboard.

"Beast, all you have to do is ask me to stay with you. You don't have to chain me up like I'm some wild animal. I'll come back to you if that's what you want," I reassure him.

My captor hesitates momentarily, but then goes back to work. He swabs the inside of my left arm with an alcohol pad before sticking me with one of the needles.

I hiss.

"I need to numb the area so I can insert the implant." It's all the explanation I get.

"Why can't I take the pill?" I ask, watching him work on my arm.

"Because pills can be forgotten. When I'm ready to fuck a baby into you, I'll do so. Until then, you will keep this implant in."

"You could always wear a condom," I tell him.

"Do I look like a man who likes to fuck with a damn rubber on? I'm the type that likes to watch my seed drip from a slutty little cunt, and that's exactly what's going to happen when we fuck."

"You're crude..."

"And you talk too much..." he counters.

"Why me?" I finally ask after all this time.

Beast only shrugs.

"How do you expect me to choose you if you won't tell me why you want me instead of somebody else?"

"You want the truth?"

I roll my eyes. "Of course."

"Your pretty little virgin pussy called out to me, and the beast in me answered it."

Surprisingly, I don't feel anything after Beast numbs my arm, and within a few minutes, the implant is in place, and he's putting a band-aid over it. He uncuffs my wrist but doesn't allow me to sit up.

"What now?" I ask, annoyed.

He doesn't say anything as he positions himself between my legs and takes me with his mouth. I moan at the way his tongue flicks back and forth over my clit before sinking into me. Only when I come does he flip me around and yanks up my hips.

"I'm going to take this, little imp. Do you have a problem with that?" Beast asks as he pushes a finger into me.

"Will you let me go back to work if I say yes?"

"Are you trying to bribe me?" A sting heats my ass as his hand comes down on it.

The burn feels so good that I wiggle my backside at him.

"Yes, I am."

Beast slips another finger into me.

"How do I know you will come back?"

"Send a driver for me. Better yet, come get me yourself. Of course, that means you will have to remove your mask..."

"I've a better idea." Beast leaves me for a few minutes, then returns with another syringe.

"What is that? Wait, what are you doing?" I shriek as he comes at me, gripping my hair and yanking my head to the side.

I feel a pinch behind my ear, and then it's over with. My hand flies to the area he just injected while I stare open-mouthed at him.

"Tracker."

"You put a freaking tracker in me?" Squealing, I jump from the bed to go to the mirror, but Beast grabs me around the waist.

I kick and punch at him, but it does no good. He throws me back on the bed, where I land on my stomach. Knowing I'll continue to fight him, he plays dirty and begins fingering me. I'm a sucker for a great fingerbang, and he knows it. All too soon, he has me moaning out his name, begging him to let me come.

"Let me come in your tight ass, and I'll let you come at the same time. How about that?"

"Fuck, yes...please, Beast!"

I even stick my ass in the air for him, reaching back and spreading my cheeks just how he likes it. However, this is the first time he'll be using his cock. He usually uses the toy on me.

"That's my good girl. Let me see that beautiful rosebud before I destroy it."

I feel his tongue first, prodding its way around my hole before he spits inside me. His zipper comes down, and his jeans rustle, and suddenly, he's there, at my entrance.

"Tell me to stop, little imp..."

"Mm, why would I do that?"

"That's what I thought," he says as he pushes his length inside me.

He takes his time, but I still feel the burn of him stretching me. It would be easier with lube, but where's the fun in that?

"Oh, yes...don't stop..."

"There's no going back now, little imp. This fine ass is mine."

When he's finally in, he gives me a brief reprieve before he pulls out and thrusts back in.

"Oh shit! You're so big, Beast."

His wicked chuckle should scare me, but it does the opposite. I don't know what it is, but I love the monster in him. He's dark and mysterious, and I need more of him. I'm pretty sure I have Stockholm Syndrome. I shouldn't be loving what my captor is doing to me, yet I crave it all.

Gripping my hair, Beast causes my back to arch so much that I can't move. All I can do is be his vessel—and I'm okay with that.

"Fuck, little imp. You're so goddamn tight!" He states through clenched teeth, and I can't help but smile.

"All the more to milk you, Beast," I muse as I squeeze my walls together.

"You've got that right—fuck!"

He punches into me repeatedly, never lessening his thrusts. A burn erupts on my shoulder blade, and I scream. The searing pain doesn't stop, and neither does Beast. It isn't until I feel wetness run down toward my shoulder that I realize he's cut me.

I try to break free of him, but he only fucks me harder, and then his mouth is on me. Beast licks and sucks at my wound while grunting and groaning. He's getting off on drinking my blood!

Why does that thought turn me on?

Beast reaches around me and starts playing with my clit while he continues to suck on my wound. This is so wrong, but how do I stop it? What if I don't want to stop it?

Beast builds the flames inside me until I can no longer hold back.

"Yes! Oh, God... yes! More Beast...give me more!"

"Come for me, imp! Come for your master..."

He pumps a few more times before thrusting deeper than ever and releasing himself. I fall over the edge with him, and we ride out the euphoric wave together.

When he pulls out, Beast orders me to stay as I am as he climbs off the bed and goes to the tray he carried in earlier. He returns with one of the bandages he had brought and applies it to my wound.

"Are you a vampire or something?" I can't believe I'm even asking him this, but...

"There's no such thing as vampires. I just love the taste of blood...It's one of my kinks."

"Oh, I see."

"Do you have a problem with that?" he asks.

"No, not really."

"Good. Wait until your cycle. It's my favorite time of the month."

His words make me want to gag, but I remain quiet. Maybe this birth control will prevent me from having my period. I know it sometimes does that, and I'm not mad about it, especially considering what I know.

"So, am I good to go to work tomorrow?"

"You'll have one task to do before you go back to work, but no worries, I've already talked to Mr. Silverman. He knows you won't be back until the beginning of the week."

"What? How did you manage that?"

"I have my connections. Now, I suggest you get some rest, because later, you'll be my date. I want you on my arm when I go upstairs. I've got business colleagues coming and I want to show you off."

Most guys would kiss their women, but not Beast. He pinches my nipple instead and chuckles before leaving me all alone once again.

FIVE

Ayla

The club is filled with masked patrons, but the atmosphere is just like every other night I've been there. The only thing different is that I'm at Beast's side. I still wear the collar with the leash, but I feel wanted as I stand beside him as his submissive.

Others come to him, but he gently pushes them aside and continues on. I'm dressed in a red body con dress that hugs every curve I have. The slits down each side showcase just enough skin without showing too much.

Thinking back to earlier, when Beast brought me the dress, his words warmed me to the core.

"Nobody will see what is mine until I'm ready to let them see it. Your body is my temple. Mine to touch and mine to worship."

A shiver passes through me just thinking about it, and Beast notices, but doesn't say or do anything. If he thinks I may be cold, he doesn't seem to care enough to warm me up. I'm okay with that, though. I'm here for his pleasure, not for him to coddle me.

I want to please him so I can go back to work and get on with my life. This is all happening so fast, and as excited as I am about the Beast choosing me, I still have responsibilities.

"Come, imp. I have to talk to a few friends of mine. I promised them I'd show you off." Beast leads us to a room where the dancers are on platforms, dancing on poles while a scene unfolds on stage.

We stop at a booth in the corner of the room where four men in masks sit, enjoying a drink and watching the performance on the stage. Unlike most, who only wear a mask covering their eyes, these men are wearing a full-face mask. Not that it matters much to me. I couldn't care less who they are. There's only one man who holds my attention, and right now, he's bringing me to stand in front of him.

"Gentlemen. I'm so glad you could make it. I hope you've all chosen someone to spend your time with later." Beast chuckles. "Of course, if you're just into each other, that's okay, too."

"You're a son of a bitch, do you know that?" One of the men says in an amused tone. "You know damn well we pick out our house subs as soon as we get here. Then again, if you've brought this beauty over to share, I might just give up my chosen and join you."

"You only wish, Drako," Beast says to the man, adding, "Nobody touches my imp. I wouldn't want her ruined before I can have her."

"My apologies, Beast. To be honest, she's a tiny thing. Is she even able to take you?" the guy muses.

All four men chuckle at what this Drako guy says, but it seems as though Beast isn't having it. Snapping his fingers, a server approaches, carrying a tray with assorted items. Beast grabs a small bottle of lube before sending the server away.

"Bend over the table, imp," he orders me.

I almost snap my head to him, but remember that I must be on my best behavior. So, taking in a much-needed breath, I rest my chest against the table in front of Beast.

Cool air hits my bare ass when my dress is lifted, exposing my backside.

"You know what to do, imp." I hear Beast say, and exhale the breath I had just taken in.

He's going to do this in front of these men? Why do I find that so fucking hot? It could be because I don't know any of these men.

"That's a good girl," Beast praises me when I reach back and spread my ass cheeks for him.

I already know he's not going to fuck my pussy, but that's okay. The thought of having his girth inside my tight back hole has me getting wet already.

Using enough lube so he can slide in easier than when he uses just his saliva, I feel a bit disappointed when I don't feel the burn. However, Beast groans as he pushes into my ass, and that alone has me moaning myself.

When he begins to really fuck me, his friends watch intensely as he takes me over the edge. I should feel ashamed to be doing this, but it's what I've always daydreamed of—being taken with onlookers. I just hadn't thought it would be this way.

"Look at all four of them as I make you come, imp." Gripping my hair, Beast yanks my head back so I have to stare at his friends.

"Oh, God, Beast...please!"

"That's right. It's my cock you're begging for, isn't it?"

"Yes, Beast..."

"Call me Daddy..."

"Yes, Daddy...please, don't stop!"

I can feel the onslaught of my climax as it begins to rise. Beast makes me come in no time as he fucks my ass hard and fast. He fills me up with his release soon after, but before he does, Beast leans over and bites my ear.

"You're being such a good girl. Tell me, imp, were you always a good girl for your real daddy?"

Why in the world would he bring up my father at a time like this? He's the last person I want to be thinking about while he fucks my back door.

"How does it feel getting this slutty little ass fucked in front of complete strangers? Does it turn you on, imp?" Beast asks louder for his friends to hear.

"Yes, Daddy..." I moan.

My mouth drops open as pleasure fills me, and I arch my back a little more as I push myself back to meet each of his thrusts.

"Isn't my little imp so tantalizing, fellas? Don't you wish you could fuck this sweet, tight hole?"

"You sure are a fucking cock tease, Beast! I'd destroy that ass and then some if you would just give me five minutes with her." One of the men to my left says, and I freeze.

Beast notices the tension coiling around me and chuckles before leaning back into my ear.

"How would Daddy feel if he knew he was talking about destroying his own daughter's ass... Hm?"

I swear my heart stops once his words register, and I look more closely at his four friends. The one, second from the left of us, does look somewhat familiar, and when he reaches for the glass in front of him, that's when I see it. The man wears the same exact watch my mother gave him for their twenty-fifth anniversary two years ago.

Oh, my God. The Beast just fucked me in front of my dad, and my father has no idea who I am! Is this why Beast insisted I wear a full-face mask, too? This is so wrong!

My body doesn't seem to care, though. It explodes with euphoric dynamite, and I scream as I squirt all over the floor. My body convulses as it continues to come, gripping Beast's cock and sending him over the edge, too.

"That's a girl. Look at that pussy leak!" the man I've learned is my father states in a salacious tone.

I want to vomit.

"Easy, imp. I may be an asshole, but I would never allow Daddy Dearest to touch you. I just want to teach him a lesson, but that's a story for another day. You've done well..."

Beast pulls himself out of me, then helps me to stand. He even goes as far as fixing my dress so it's covering my ass once more. The man I once thought was a God has now changed into Satan himself.

Who would do that to someone?

Beast says his goodbyes to his friends and then, taking the leash in a tight grip, he walks us to the doorway leading out of the room. However, he stops and glances back to where we had left his friends. I remain looking forward, but I don't miss the dark and warped smirk lifting his lips through his mask. Without any warning, Beast reaches up and rips the mask off my face and tosses it to the floor.

"Be a good girl and smile at the camera for me, little imp." Beast nods to the security camera in the corner of the room we've just walked into.

Doing as I'm told, I then look to the floor, ashamed of what just transpired. Ashamed because even though that was so-so wrong, I find the action itself to be so damn hot—Beast taking me as he had, right there. Had it not been my father sitting there, I'd be on cloud nine.

"Hey," Beast lifts my chin, forcing me to look at him when he says, "If you want to be by my side in the club, you will hold your head high and be proud of everything that I decide to do to this delectable body of yours."

"Yes, Beast."

He shoves his thumb between my teeth and pulls down, opening my mouth wide. He spits.

"You are mine, and your actions reflect upon me. I don't want people thinking that the woman I've chosen to be by my side is a meek fucking little mouse. You're far from being one, and I want you to act like it."

His words surprise me. I didn't realize he saw me as a fierce woman, at least not by how he's treated me lately. The collar and the leash tell a different story. He said it was so I wouldn't run away, but if he keeps the door locked to the room I'm in, how can I leave? I honestly thought he was trying to break me, but now I'm just confused.

SIX

Beast

It was a dick move, but I've never claimed to be a nice guy. In fact, I'm far from it. I may have become enamored by Ayla Kennedy, but I haven't forgotten why I went searching for her in the first place.

All she was supposed to be was the name of someone close to another person on my shit list. Who knew I would find the woman who would become the perfect plaything for my inner beast?

I don't think my fucking Ayla's ass right there in front of her father bothered her as much as she wants me to believe. Yeah, she may not like the fact that her father was there, but being fucked in front of my friends turned her on. I doubt she would have come as hard as she did had it bothered her more.

Pressing send on that email I will be sending out with the video later will be the icing on my cake. I look forward to seeing the response I receive when I do so.

I walk my little imp back to her room, and I lock the door behind us. Leaning against the solid oak structure, I drop the leash and free her from my grasp as I watch her closely.

Ayla stands in the middle of the room, not sure of what she should be doing. I decide to help her out, and I push away from the door.

Strolling over to her, I take her chin and tilt her face up. Her bright blue eyes still burn with lust as she gazes back at me.

"You did well, little imp. I want to reward you," I tell my little plaything.

Hope springs to her eyes, and her words rush out. "I can go back to work tomorrow!"

I burst her bubble by shaking my head. "No, not yet."

I'm not ready to share her with the world yet, and I'm still unsure whether she will come back to me if I give her what she wants. I don't like to see the light fade from her eyes, but it's inevitable.

"I want you to look around this room and find something you really like." I can see I've confused her with my request, so I add, "Amuse me, will you?"

Her brows form a crease between them as she bites her lip, then searches her surroundings. Ayla wanders around the cave-like room, picking up different items and running her fingers over other items.

She stops at the bamboo vase on the table where I keep my switches. Picking it up, she slides her hand over the smooth surface, then turns to me.

"This is beautiful. Where did you find it?" she asks softly.

Going over and standing beside her, I take the wooden vase from her and pull out all the switches, placing them on the table.

"I found it while traveling and thought it would make a great addition to this room. You've chosen well, little imp. Go lie down on the bed."

Her eyes snap to mine. "What are—"

I cut her off with a raise of my brow. "Are you questioning me, imp?"

She wants to say more, but instead, she shakes her head and walks over to the bed. Sitting on the edge, Ayla then slides herself back before lying down.

There's a slight tremble to her legs, which I love to see, but they're not trembling enough. I'll remedy that momentarily.

Removing my evening jacket, I then roll up my sleeves, showing off the veins in my forearms. I move to the table next to the bed and open the drawer to grab what I'll need.

Placing it and the vase down on the bed, I reach over, taking hold of the top of Ayla's dress and tearing it down the middle, baring her beautiful body to me.

"You won't be needing this anymore. I like you naked anyway," I tell her when she gasps. "Open your legs, imp, and play with yourself until I'm ready."

40

Eying the items suspiciously, her hand moves between her legs, and she does as she's told. Ayla rubs her clit a few times before slipping a finger inside of her. It's a gorgeous sight, but not as gorgeous as it's going to be in a moment.

Picking up the bamboo vase, I uncap the bottle of lube I grabbed from the dresser and squirt a generous amount on the base. I won't use the opening, because I don't want to cause a suction inside and hurt her. Although my little imp probably wouldn't mind that so much.

I wrap my hand around the base and begin stroking the long cylinder. The radius of the vase is about two inches, and it stands about fifteen inches tall. Of course, Ayla won't be able to take all of it, but she's going to eat up a good portion of it.

I watch as Ayla pleasures herself, and I find myself hardening. I'm not sure what makes me do it, but I hover over her momentarily before pressing my lips against hers. It's hard doing it through the mask, but I'm successful at pulling a moan from her lips, nevertheless. When I pull away from her, I glance between us at her hand pumping in and out of her, and I can no longer wait.

"Move your hand, imp. I'm ready."

Ayla's fingers immediately go into her mouth and are sucked on, but regardless of how fucking hot that is, she did not have permission.

My hand comes down hard on her clit as I slap her. Again and again, my hand punishes her before I growl out, "You greedy little imp. I didn't say you could have that. Your essence belongs to me!"

"I'm sorry, Beast. You make me lose my head sometimes..."

"Well, maybe I won't reward you with a good fucking," I say as I hold up the readied vase.

The relief that washes over her face at hearing that raises my eyebrow. Maybe I can still get off from watching me fuck her with the vase, knowing it's more of a punishment than a reward.

I love using unusual items to fuck a nice pussy. It's always fascinated me how many things can get a woman off.

"Hold your legs up and wide. Offer me this greedy little thing and I'll decide whether to punish it or pleasure it," I order gruffly.

My cock is still hard and will need its own release soon. However, my mind forgets about my needs the moment I glance down at my little imp offering herself to me.

Very slowly, I slide two fingers into her sopping wet cunt and pump them in and out before scissoring them to stretch her out further. It isn't until I insert the third, and then the fourth, that I feel her readiness. I want so badly to maneuver my hand and slide my thumb inside, too—fisting her. I know she'll take it like the good girl she is. Maybe one day soon.

Removing my fingers, I bring the base of the wooden vase to her opening and slowly work it inside of her. Her hands fist the bedding as her body tenses, causing me to stop all movement.

"If you want it to hurt, then by all means, stay tense. The more you relax, the more you will enjoy it." I wait until I see her body begin to relax. "Play with your nipples and rub your clit—it will help."

"I don't think I want this reward, Beast," my little imp states hesitantly.

A wicked grin spreads across my face. "This is no longer a reward. You were a naughty girl, and since you really don't want this, it's your punishment. You can either take this and have the option to enjoy it, or you can feel the switch as it reddens that beautiful ass. It's your choice. Either ask me to fuck you or whip you. Either way, you will be receiving your punishment."

Worrying her bottom lip for a few seconds, she finally says, "Fuck me, Beast."

"It will be my pleasure..." I push the vase in further, watching her channel expand.

A woman's body should be the Eighth Wonder of the World. The things it can do are simply amazing.

In and out I thrust the vase, twisting and turning it as Ayla plays with herself. Soon enough, I have my imp moaning and humping the bamboo like it's my fucking cock.

"God, you're such a slut, aren't you?" I ask.

"Yes, Beast! I'm your slut..."

"That's right. If I let you go back to work, you will come back, won't you? Not because I tell you to, but because your body now knows who it belongs to. You will come back because you're a slut for my cock and you haven't even had it inside this tight cunt of yours yet."

"Yes!" Ayla cries out as she fucks the vase harder.

I can't hold it in any longer. Ayla looks fucking perfect as she fucks the vase, and I need a release, so I climb to my knees and let my throbbing cock out. I stroke it up and down, moving faster, and I fuck my little imp faster.

"Come for me, imp. Be the dirty little whore that I know you to be and come all over my expensive vase. Let your essence soak into the bamboo, so it's forever a part of it." When she doesn't come right away, I demand, "Slap that clit..."

She does, and it's all it takes.

Seeing her come around the vase sends me spiraling, and I roar as ribbons of cum shoot out, landing on Ayla's stomach and pubic area. It's never-ending.

"Fuck!" I curse, pumping my dick into my hand harder until every last drop is out.

SEVEN

Ayla

"Wake up, little imp. Otherwise, you're going to be late," Beast's voice is low, and sounds smooth as silk as he wakes me up.

Opening my eyes, I blink rapidly until they come into focus on his magnificent frame. His dark hair is messy as always, and the browns of his eyes peek out from the mask.

I wish I knew what he looked like. Not that it really matters because even without knowing what he looks like, I'm too addicted to him. He can be as hideous as they come, and I will still kneel at his feet and beg him to fuck me.

"Hm," I hum as I stretch my arms over my head. "Late for what?"

"Well, work, of course. Unless you no longer want to go. I'm more than willing to leave you chained up and keep you as my sex slave," he says, amused.

I shoot up into a sitting position, not caring that the blanket falls, baring my breasts to him. My pulse starts to race, scared that this is some kind of joke. It's been a few days since Beast took me into the club and fucked me in front of my father. I've been on my best behavior this whole time.

"Are you fucking with me, Beast? Please don't tease me..." I plead desperately.

"You've been a good girl, imp, and with the tracker in you, I'm confident that you will come back to me and not run," he states, running his hand through my hair until he gets to my nape. He then tugs it, making my head tilt back. "If you try, you won't like the outcome."

"I can't leave you even if I wanted to."

"Why is that?"

I nibble on my lower lip for a second, trying to decide if I should tell him or if I should lie.

Fuck it.

I decide to go with the truth and say, "Because my soul calls out for you. I don't think I can go without being with you, Beast."

"Is that so?" His lips twitch under the mask.

"Yes..." I whisper my reply.

I never should have said what I just let slip.

"Poor little imp. I feel sorry for you," he tells me.

"Why is that?"

"Because what you're saying speaks of love, and my soul is damned—there is no room for love."

"Does it?" I ask. "I mean, speak of love."

I've never been in love before. All I know is that when this man leaves me all alone, my soul weeps in his absence. It hurts to be away from him. I'm not sure how work will pan out because of it, but maybe it will help.

"It sounds that way. However, it makes no difference to me. You're mine, regardless. If you feel the need to love me, then so be it. Just don't expect it in return."

"I see..."

"Trust me, imp. You don't want me to love you. You just need me to make you come repeatedly until you're far out in subspace. Then you'll want me to do it again."

"Is that all you think of me? Someone to please and use as a cum dumpster?" I ask, trying to act insulted.

"Mm...you love when I use you like that, imp. I think being my plaything is all you ever wanted. Tell me I'm wrong."

I push away from him without answering. I can't deny what he's saying because it's the truth. Not just anyone can treat me the way he does. There's just something about the way he goes about using me for his needs, yet he still pleases me in the process, which has me panting after him constantly.

He doesn't treat me delicately like others would. No, that's not how the Beast works, and he doesn't give a shit. It's one of the reasons why I was drawn to him the first time I saw him here at the club.

He grabs my ankle and pulls me to the edge of the bed. I hear the zipper to his pants, and I stop fighting.

"Don't fucking move. If you're going in to work, then you're going to be leaking my cum so others know that you are off limits."

"My ass is still sore from last night, Beast..."

"I'm done waiting. I want what is now mine, and I'm not waiting another day," Beast growls, and then he's pushing into me.

"Uh..." I moan.

He feels so different than the dildos and vibrators I've used. His length alone is so much more than I'm used to taking, and it feels as though he's entering parts he shouldn't be entering.

"Fuck, little imp. This cunt is so fucking tight. I'm afraid I may destroy it this morning..."

"Do it..." I say, moaning some more.

Beast snickers.

"Always a needy little slut for me, aren't you, little imp."

"Yes, Beast... just for you."

"That's my good girl..."

Beast wasn't lying when he said he was going to destroy me this morning. He pounded my virgin pussy as though it had taken plenty of cocks. Having a real one inside me, though, feels nothing like I thought it would.

Because Beast is so big, he stretched and bruised my insides with every thrust, and I loved every minute of it. When he came, it wasn't just inside me. He made sure to pull out, flip me over, and sprayed the rest of it on my chest and stomach. He then proceeded to rub it into my skin as if it were lotion, and then told me to get dressed.

After a night of getting fucked in the ass and then this morning's little romp, Beast denied me a shower until I came home after work. Only then am I to clean myself of his claiming.

I should be appalled or, at the very least, disgusted with the idea of wearing a man's bodily fluids all over me, but I'm not. It fills me with a sense of being owned. Knowing that someone wants me enough to mark me the way Beast did just so nobody would touch me makes me feel giddy.

Some brickhouse by the name of Rocko drives me to work. He's full of tattoos and scars, with a nose that appears to have been broken a few times. I've seen him at The Lair, working as security, so it makes sense that Beast would use him to be my bodyguard.

I still find it weird having one, but if I've learned anything in the little time I've been with the Beast, it's that you don't argue. His word is law.

The moment the doors to the elevator open, I'm met with a warm smile from Amilia. I was so worried about coming up with an excuse for my absences, but it seems there was no need. Amilia gets up and comes around her desk, holding her arms open for me.

"You poor girl! I heard all about the death of your grandmother. That must have been so hard on you. I hope you know that I'm keeping you in my prayers."

"Thank you," I say, hugging her back and trying not to sound confused.

So, Beast called me out for a death in the family...hmm.

"Did you receive the flowers Mr. Silverman sent to the funeral home?" Amilia asks, holding me at arm's length.

"I did," I lie. "It was so thoughtful of him. I hope he wasn't too upset over me missing as many days as I did."

Amilia steps back, waving my concern off. "Of course, he wasn't. He understands that you had to fly out west for the funeral. After all, she was like a mother to you—she raised you after all."

Wow. Beast really gave them a good story. Still, I feel so bad having missed so many days, and I say as much.

"Well, I just hope my absence didn't make Mr. Silverman's job harder on him. I know how busy he is."

"Pfft..." Amilia returns to her desk. "He's barely been here himself. He booked a few meetings while you were gone, so you really didn't miss much. I'm sure he recorded each one, so you can go over them."

Hearing this makes me feel a little better, and I give Amilia a smile. "Okay, well, I had better get to my desk then and get to work."

Rocko never got off the elevator, so luckily, I didn't have to explain who he was. That would have been a little strange for Amilia to see, and not something I would have enjoyed explaining.

I can see the elevator from my office, so when Mr. Silverman arrives, I jump up and hurry to the coffee pot to grab his morning coffee. I hadn't seen any work on my desk when I arrived, so I've just been sitting here waiting for my boss to come in.

I knock on his half-closed door, and I hear his gruff response, "Come in."

"Good morning, Mr. Silverman. I would like to apologize for taking—"

"Don't..." he cuts me off.

"Pardon? Don't what?" I ask, confused.

"Don't apologize. Shit happens, and people die. You're back, now get your head in the game, and do your job." Not once does Mr. Silverman glance at me as he rummages through the files on his desk.

"Oh, okay. Um, Amilia said that you may have some recordings from meetings that you attended, for me to go through. I can get started on them—"

"I don't," he cuts me off again. My boss then holds out a few folders toward me and informs me, "I need these numbers by lunchtime. Don't be late..."

"Yes, Sir. I'll get them done immediately." I turn and rush out of his office and back to my desk.

That was the most uncomfortable few minutes I've ever had. Mr. Silverman must have woken up on the wrong side of the bed—he's cranky as hell.

My boss's sour disposition motivates me to get him the numbers as soon as possible. Once done, I look at the clock and see that it's only five minutes until noon, and I breathe a sigh of relief.

I walk the files back to his office, and since his door is wide open, I just walk in. I hold the files out for him, but he taps his desk right beside him. The problem is, his desk is wide, so I have to walk all the way around it just to place them in the spot he indicated.

I do just that, but when I try to move away, his hand whips out, keeping me in place.

"Sir?" I question.

"What is that smell?" he asks, furrowing his brows.

I lift my nose to the air and sniff, but all I can smell is his sexy musk cologne.

"I don't smell anything, Sir."

Mr. Silverman pulls me closer and sniffs me—*me*—and then the most embarrassing thing happens. My boss makes a sour face and shoves me away.

"I suggest you shower before coming into work, Miss Kennedy. I don't like my employees smelling like a whorehouse. You're done for the day. Go home and clean yourself up..."

He then returns to his work, and I rush from his office, mortified by what just took place. Beast knew what he was doing, but damn it, there was no reason to be jealous of my boss!

Shaking uncontrollably as I enter the elevator, I text Rocko to meet me in front of the building, and then I lean against the wall and close my eyes. *I'll never live this down.*

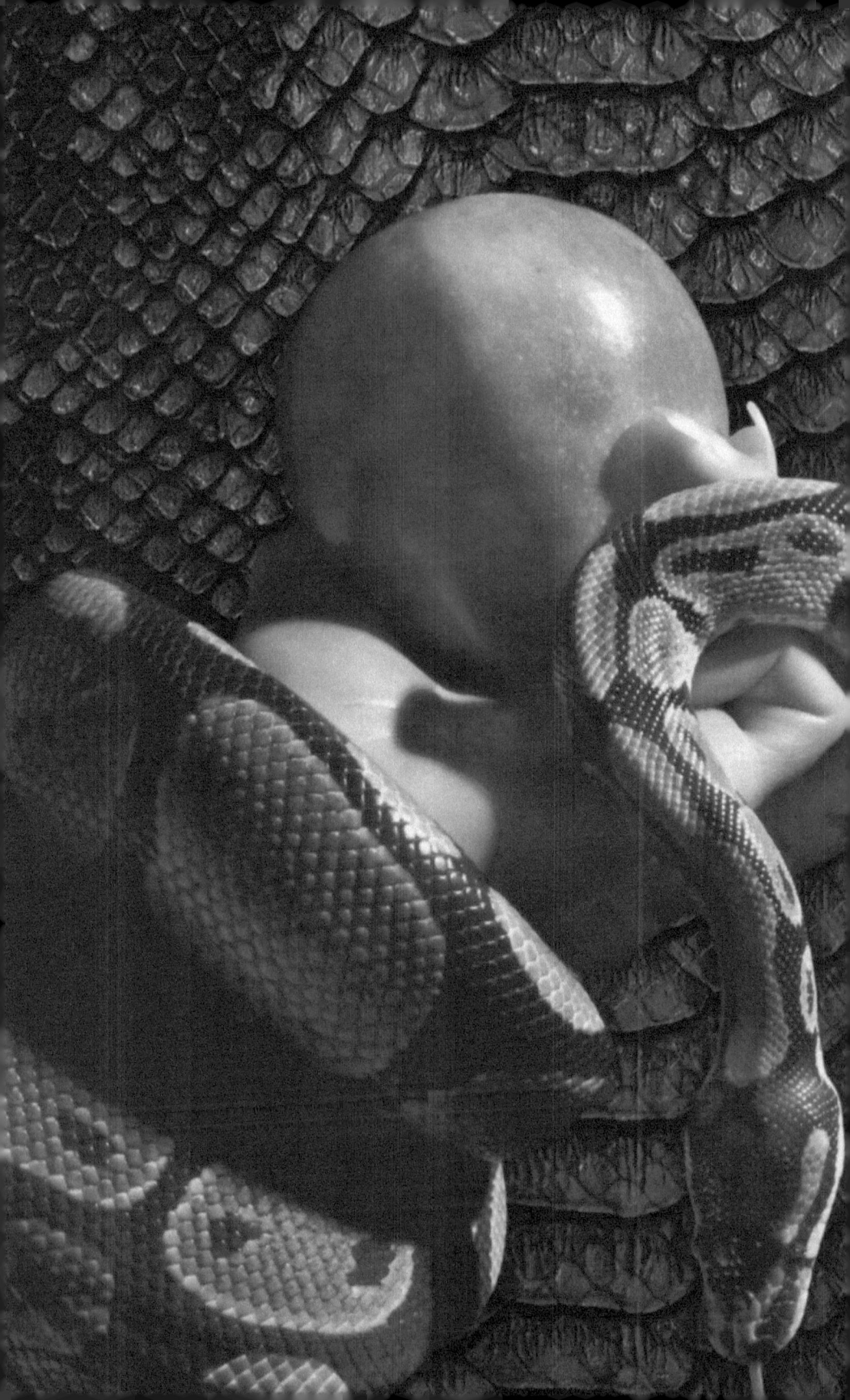

EIGHT

Beast

My phone vibrates on my desk, and I pick it up to see Rocko's name pop up. Swiping right, I answer, "Yeah."

"Miss Kennedy texted me. She wants me to meet her out front of the building," Rocko states gruffly.

"Thanks for informing me. Bring her straight to The Lair, no stops along the way," I instruct.

"Will do, Sir."

I hang up, smirking. Oh, she's going to be pissed, and I'm here for it. I knew what I was doing this morning when I marked her. My plan is going accordingly. Now, to run a little errand and get back to the club, so I can have a little fun with my little imp.

I've got a guy who specializes in making one-of-a-kind restraints, and he called me this morning to inform me that my special order was ready. Because my little imp loves pain and is so needy for it, I've had a special harness prepared for her.

The harness is to be worn at all times. It delivers electrical currents whenever I choose, controlled by a remote. With rings positioned all around it, I can cuff my little imp to it in any arrangement I want. My favorite part is the nipple clamps, but those will come later.

Carrying the bag with my special order inside, I enter The Lair. The club isn't open at the moment, but employees are bustling around, preparing for tonight's shows. There's nothing special going on tonight, but it's always hectic when opening a kink club nightly.

The Lair is the cleanest club you will ever see in these parts. I don't stand for anything less than spotless. Of course, bodily fluids may be spilled here and there, but I have employees go around and clean it all up immediately. You can eat off the floors in my club, which some submissives do at their Dom's orders.

Rocko is sitting at the bar, watching a race on the television, while the head bartender ensures all is in order behind the bar. I clap Rocko on the shoulder, and he gives me his attention.

"How's my little pet doing?"

Rocko shrugs. "Miss Kennedy seemed a little pissy on the ride home. She kept sniffing herself for some odd reason."

Smirking, I nod.

"I had better go and tend to her then. Thanks for driving her. Same time tomorrow."

"Yes, Boss."

Rocko's a good man. He's a scary-looking motherfucker, but he's good shit. He's one of the few men that I trust these days.

I walk through the halls where most of the private rooms are, and then through the voyeur gallery. Pulling my keys from my pocket, I unlock the door that leads to The Cave—my very own special room.

I stand outside the room, peering through the two-way mirror. My little imp can't see me, but I can see her. She's wrapped in a towel, sitting on the edge of the bed, biting her thumbnail.

Glancing at the bag in my hand, I visualize the harness wrapped around my imp's chest, and my dick hardens. The way Ayla is going to look in this black leather strap, with her tits squeezed through the breast holes, may be my undoing. I guess we're about to find out.

I grab the mask hanging just outside the door and pull it on over my head. I remove my shirt and hang it on the hook from which I just pulled my mask before unlocking the door. I enter and find Ayla's blue eyes staring back at me.

"You're back early. Did you miss me that much, little imp?"

She scoffs. "You wish."

I frown and nod at the towel. "Did you disobey me and shower?"

Ayla lifts her chin, defiantly, and says, "Yes, I did. My boss could smell me and ordered me to go home and shower because I smelled like a whorehouse! It was so humiliating!"

I move to stand before her, gripping her chin between my fingers. "That's what it was meant for. I want everyone to know that you are off limits because this cunt is already taken."

The way my little imp melts in my hand at my words, it's as if I just praised her and called her a good girl. My imp has realized a lot about herself, but I don't think she's come to the conclusion that she loves to be degraded and humiliated. It's new to her, but that's what I'm here for. By the time I'm done with Ayla Kennedy, she'll be so dependent on this lifestyle that she will never want to leave.

"I've got a present for you, but now I don't think you deserve it. You disobeyed me and showered before I gave you permission," I tell her, holding up the bag.

My little imp opens her towel and goes to her knees before me, bowing her head.

"I am sorry, Beast. I deserve to be punished for my disobedience. It will never happen again."

"Hm, what sort of punishment do you feel you deserve?" I ask, setting the bag down on the floor and crossing my arms in front of my chest.

I wait for Ayla to think of something, but the longer I wait, the more impatient I become. Circling around her as she kneels on the floor, I think to myself. Something comes to mind, and I doubt she will consent to it, but then again, it *is* supposed to be a punishment.

"Maybe you're not cut out to be by my side. Perhaps we should throw in the towel and go our separate ways. I'm sure I'll find the perfect submissive to meet all of my needs..."

Ayla's head snaps up.

"What? No...please! I'll be better, Beast. I don't want to leave. I want you to teach me more—I *need* you to teach me how to be the perfect sub for you."

"Will you obey me and take your punishment like a good girl?" I ask.

"Yes, Beast."

"I'll let you know now, it's going to hurt. But once we finish,"—I squat before her and push two fingers into her already wet cunt—"I will make this naughty girl weep all over."

"Uh...yes, Beast..." my little imp moans as my fingers stretch her out.

I pick up the pace, punching my fingers in and out, and just when she's about to come, I retract them. Licking each digit clean of her essence, my little imp whimpers at the loss of them.

"Stand," I order.

She does so, hastily, making me smirk.

I reach down, grab the bag I brought with me, and pull out the black leather harness. I hold the strappy item up for her to see, but she says nothing.

"Arms out in front of you, imp."

"Why do you call me that?" she asks as I slide the straps over her arms.

As I adjust the harness over her breasts, ensuring it's the right fit, I then circle around Ayla and fasten it in the back. There's a lock on the collar, so only I can remove it.

"Because, you, my little devilish nympho, are like a little sprite. They're cute, but beware because they can be very mischievous and vicious. Like a little demon or fiend."

She smiles at my explanation, and I'm unsure whether that's a good or bad thing. It's not meant to be a compliment, but hell, if she might be taking it as one.

I come back to stand in front of her and tug at her nipples. Her breasts are like balls sticking out of the harness, and her nips are right there for all to see. I should pierce those babies sometime.

"You look like the perfect little whore for me, imp. Tell me, are you going to act like one, too?"

"If that's what pleases you, Beast."

"What pleases me is when others know that *you are mine!*" I grab the silver ring on her collar and pull her to the other side of the room, where a padded table sits.

Lifting her, I set her on top and shove her down to her back. I take her first arm and secure it, before moving down to her leg, and then over to the other side. By the time I've finished securing my imp to the table, she's breathing heavily.

"What I'm about to do is going to make you want to move and struggle, but know this, if you do either, I will click on this..." I hold the remote for the harness up so she can see it.

"What happens when you click that?" she asks, shakily.

The grin I toss her is not one of amusement, but of delight because I'm dying to hear her squeal. Should I demonstrate it now, or let her get worked up over not knowing?

The former wins out, and I press the button on the remote. My little imp's body jerks and seizes just a tad as she cries out.

"Have you ever seen a shock collar for a dog? Well, I thought it would be nice to have a harness made up for you with the same concept."

Removing my finger from the button, I let her catch her breath while I go to the cabinet and pull out the other items I'm going to need. By the time I have everything set up, Ayla is breathing normal again and watching me with round eyes.

Holding up the gun in my hand, I smile at my adorably frightened imp and ask, "Are you ready?"

NINE

Ayla

Why am I so turned on at the thought of being shocked by this man? The electrical volts weren't too bad, but the way my body seized up at the press of a button, leaving me incapacitated, that is what has my lady bits dripping.

To know that he can render me immobile like that sends tingles throughout my body. Something is seriously wrong with me. Perhaps, subconsciously, I know he won't hurt me, and that's why my body responds this way. However, I really don't know too much about the Beast, not really, but honestly—that fact turns me on, too.

I yank at the restraints the Beast has secured around my limbs. Not because I want to be freed, but to ensure I can't break free. Whatever the Beast has in store for me has got to be big. Otherwise, he wouldn't bother with the restraints.

"Are you ready?" Beast's deep voice reaches me, and I let my gaze fall on him.

My breath catches when I see him hold up a tattoo gun. The sight unnerves me. I've always prided myself on not following the herd and marking my body up with ink. There's no judgment for others who like tattoos, but I've never been one to want any.

I shake my head.

"No, I don't want a tattoo, Beast!" This time, when I yank on the restraints, it's because I want to be freed. "Red!"

Beast chuckles, but stops his advancement. He tilts his head and studies me for a moment, but then pulls a cart closer. There's a little cup of black goo, which I assume is the ink. Beast sets the gun down beside it before moving to the end of the table I'm strapped to and fiddles with something underneath.

Suddenly, the table below my legs separates, spreading my legs wide. Fear takes hold.

"Beast—I said *red!* I don't want this!"

"There are no safe words between us, imp. You belong to me, which means this body belongs to me, and I'll mark it up as I see fit," Beast replies, coming back around to the cart beside me.

A tear slips free. I fucking hate needles, and Beast knows that. He figured that out when he gave me the birth control shot. It must be why he thought it best to strap me down this time.

Using his thumb, Beast wipes the single tear away as he says, "Punishments aren't meant to be enjoyed. I know you love yours, so I had to think outside the box. Since you can't follow a simple instruction like not showering my seed from your body, then I'll mark you permanently."

"What? Beast no! I promise I won't do it again..." I beg.

"Shh... Don't make me gag you, too, little imp." He moves over to a chest of drawers and returns with a vibrator with straps. "I'll be nice and make sure you feel excellent while I leave my mark. How about that?"

"Beast..." I start to say, then let my words trail off as he slides the toy inside me and turns it on.

Strapping it around my legs, so he doesn't have to hold it, Beast then gets to work on preparing for my tattoo. I moan as the vibrations change on their own, a pulsing vibe reaching the inner parts that have me already coming.

Beast chuckles as he gets comfortable between my legs with the tattoo gun in hand. Cleaning the area just above my clit, I freeze at the realization of *where* he's placing his mark. There's no use in pleading with him to stop—all I can do is prepare myself for the pain of the needle.

A buzzing noise starts up, and I hold my breath as I close my eyes. Yelping when I feel teeth nip my clit, and I lift my head to stare down at the Beast.

"Relax, or it will hurt more," Beast growls. "I'm going to bite this pretty little clit every time I feel you tense up."

Taking a few deep breaths, I can feel my body begin to relax. The vibrator, still pulsing against me, plays its part in doing so. A moan slips out as another orgasm builds.

A chuckle comes from between my legs, and my eyes meet Beast's again. He rubs my clit this time, as he taunts, "This greedy pussy knows what she wants. Stop fighting it, imp. Listen to her, and all will be fine."

I nibble my lower lip and, finally, I nod.

A slight burning sensation begins as Beast starts my punishment. I've seen tattoos done before, and I'm fairly certain a template or stencil is usually used. However, Beast doesn't use one—he's doing it by hand, which only has me guessing as to what he's marking me with.

Surprisingly, it didn't hurt as much as I thought it would, and it was over in no time at all. Beast wipes the area, and I can see him grinning through his mask.

"Beast?"

He glances up at me. "Yes?"

"When can I see your face?"

"When I feel you're deserving of it, little imp."

My mouth opens to say more, but then I snap it shut when Beast repositions my legs by moving the table again. *How many positions can this table change into?*

With my knees now bent and my legs wide open, my pulse begins to race as Beast undoes his belt and opens his pants. I watch in anticipation, my tongue gliding over my lips, as I watch him pull his cock out and palm it.

Beast strokes his hard length up and down slowly as he stares down at his work.

"This needy little pussy is Beast's property," he states while removing the straps and vibrator from my body.

Beast then positions himself at my opening and fixes his dark stare on me. It's as though he's waiting for me to deny his words, so I do what feels right to me, and I nod.

"It belongs to you, Beast."

61

Beast growls as he thrusts into me over and over, fucking me in such a primal way that I toss my head from side to side, crying out for more. His hands grip my thighs so tightly, I know his fingerprints will be visible later on. It's just another imprint this man is leaving behind.

It's not enough that he's already left one on my soul, but he feels the need to mark my body as well, and I'm not mad about it. I could have gone without the tattoo, but what's done is done, and I genuinely feel like I'm his now.

"Oh fuck, Beast! Harder! Please... Make it hurt!" I beg as he unleashes the monster inside of him.

He reaches up and slaps my left breast. "Don't tell your master what to do. I'll decide how hard I fuck *my* cunt. You just lay there and take it like a good little whore."

Oh, fuck! I love it when he gets in this mood.

I know if I antagonize him, he will do worse to me, and I can't wait to find out. So, being a glutton for punishment, I keep at it.

"But I need more! I know you can do better—"

My body seizes up as the harness strapped around me lights up with electrical bolts. Beast continues to fuck me through it, roaring as he does so.

"Fuck yes! I feel that, imp. I feel the electricity through your greedy little cunt, and it feels phenomenal!"

He lights me up again and again until we both explode in a chorus of climaxes and curse words. It's such a euphoric experience that I never want to end, but unfortunately, it does.

Beast cleans my tattoo area once again and places a clear plastic-like wrap over it.

"I'll clean this when needed. Do not touch it; it's mine to take care of," Beast tells me gruffly.

"Okay..."

I'm still breathless from our little fuck session. I just watch as Beast moves around while putting things back in their place. Beast has yet to release me from my bindings, so I wait patiently.

Finally, when everything is in its rightful place, I'm released and picked up from the table. Beast carries me over to the bed and attaches the chain to my collar, making me a prisoner once again.

"Why must you chain me like a dog?" I mutter out my question.

"Because it turns me on to see you like this." Beast pushes hair away from my face. "When I feel the time is right, we will get rid of the chain—for the most part. I'll still want to see you chained and at my mercy on occasion, but not all the time."

Beast brings me a hand mirror and places it in front of my groin area. I study his mark and nod. There's not much I can do about it now.

The words *This Needy Little Pussy Is Beast's Property* stand out just above my clit. A warmth envelopes my chest, and I smile. *I'm his.*

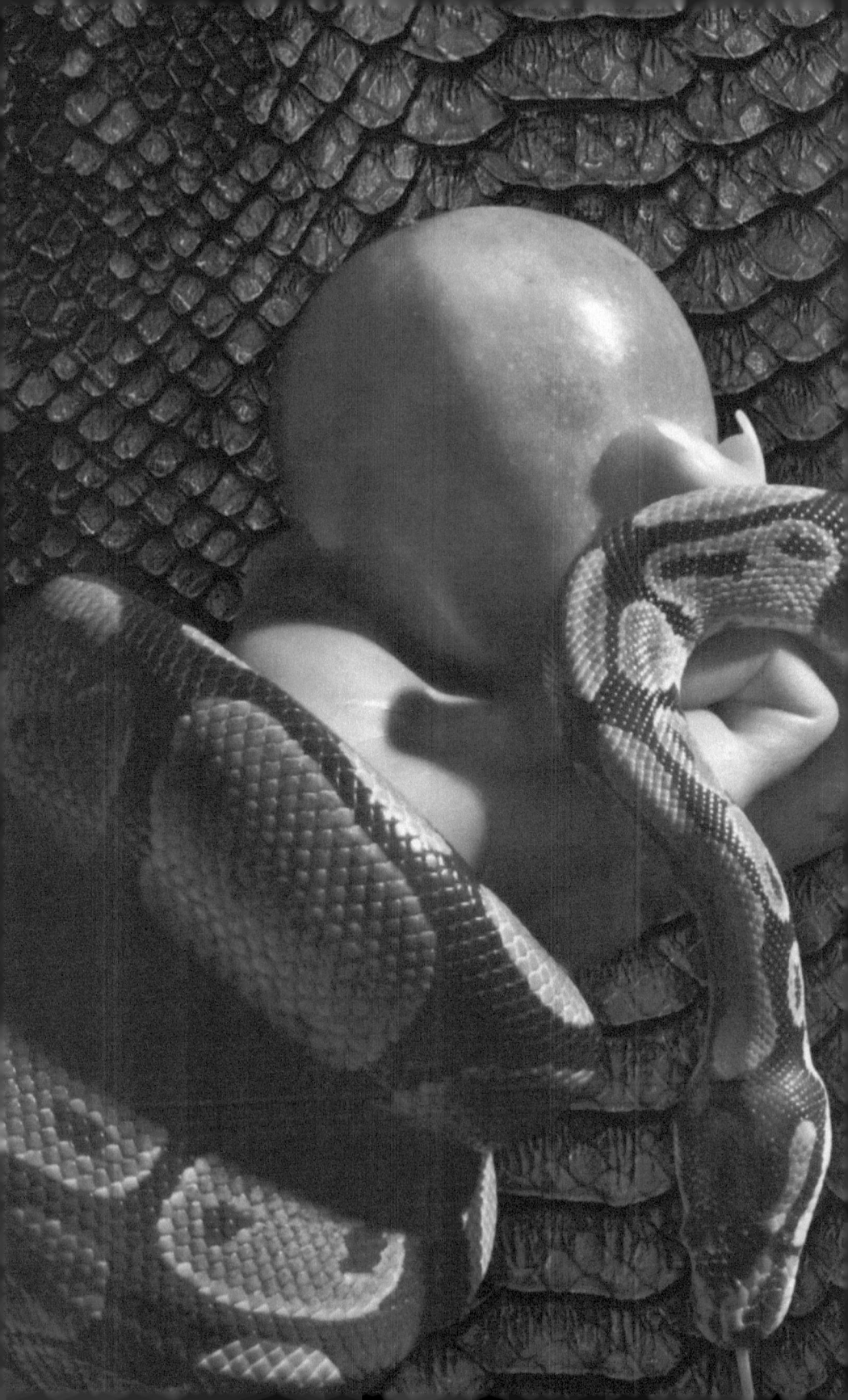

Beast

Why do those words sound so right? Of course, my little imp is mine. She's my captive, my submissive, my naughty little slut—to do with as I please—but this feeling is so much more. It's almost like she's—my *everything.*

Ayla Kennedy is my perfect match, and I'm going to make sure that I not only get my revenge but that I make her mine in every way. I left her in her room, collared and chained as always. The faster she realizes that she's mine, the faster we can move on to bigger and better *adventures.*

A knock sounds at my office door while I stand at my window, looking out at the darkness beyond. I turn to find Rocko standing just outside, and I motion for him to enter.

"He's back, Sir," my man states.

He doesn't have to tell me who he's talking about because I already know. It's the one person who always seems to want what I have. I knew that by showing off my pretty little imp the other night that he'd be back.

He's a perverse motherfucker, and if he only knew that the hard-on he's got is for his own daughter, well, that's a reveal that I can't wait to be a part of. I ought to slice his dick up for even salivating over what's mine, but I like the game I'm playing, so I'll set aside my bloodlust for the time being.

"Has he asked for anything?" I ask Rocko, turning back to stare into the darkness.

"He asked Blake where the new girl was, but Blake wasn't sure who he was talking about," Rocko replies.

Of course, the bartender wouldn't know who he's talking about, at least not this one. He wasn't working that night and has yet to see Ayla.

Nodding, I toss over my shoulder, "I'll be there in just a few minutes."

I see Rocko nod in the window's reflection before he turns and disappears. A smug grin appears on my lips as an idea develops. I spin, and, grabbing my mask, I leave my office and head to my favorite room.

Opening the door, I find my perfect little slut asleep on top of the blankets. She's wearing a sheer, babydoll nightie over her harness and is not wearing panties. I agreed to the nightie as long as it didn't keep me from seeing everything that belongs to me.

Ayla sleeps on her stomach, one knee bent, showing me *my* pretty pussy. Smirking, I go to the drawer that holds all my favorite gags and pull out the open-mouth one. I then find the arm cuffs and the butt plug with the red gem before moving to the bed.

Retrieving the lube from the drawer of the nightstand, I then spread my imp's ass cheeks and spit on her tight hole. She stirs but doesn't wake up. A slight moan slips from her lips as I squirt some lube onto her ass, but it isn't until I press a finger into her ass that her eyes slowly open.

"Mm... Beast?"

"Yes, little imp?"

"Are you going to fuck me?"

"No," I reply, chuckling. "It seems we have a visitor who wants to see more of you. I'm just getting you ready. Relax for me—I need to plug you up."

Like a good girl, Ayla relaxes and allows me to push two more fingers into her until I know she's ready. I then insert the plug and slap her ass.

Before she can turn around, I take one of her arms and secure it in the arm cuff, then do the same with the other. I lean forward, brushing her hair away from her face, and press my lips to the corner of her mouth.

"You're so beautiful when I have you all restrained. Open that gorgeous cock-sucking mouth for me, imp," I order, and she does precisely that.

There's no fighting with Ayla, and I think that's why I feel that she's the right one for me. I was her first, and I'm going to make it so I'm her last.

Placing the mouth gag into her mouth and behind her teeth, I secure the strap behind her head. Turning her, I spit into her mouth.

"You're fucking mine, remember that, imp. No one else will ever touch you without my permission. Nod if you understand."

She nods.

"Good girl. Rocko will be in to get you shortly. He'll bring a mask and put it on you before carrying you out to the club." Standing, I leave her as she is and make my way out to the bar area.

"Kennedy—I hear you're asking around about one of the new girls. Is it one in particular or just one you haven't stuck your dick in yet?" I take the stool beside the man, and Blake sets a glass down in front of me.

"You know me too well, Beast. I was hoping you were through with that pretty young thing from the other night. I've been hard for her ever since you put on that little show for us."

"Yeah, about her. I've decided that I'm going to keep her. Her tight cunt and ass are too delectable to give up. Besides, don't you have a daughter her age?"

Kennedy scoffs. "You wouldn't catch my Ayla slutting it up in a club like this. She's a good girl—you should know that."

"Hm, that I do," I reply. Spotting Rocko, I slap Kennedy's shoulder, grinning. "Speaking of my girl..."

Rocko is carrying Ayla over his shoulder just like I instructed him to. Her ass peeks out from under the nightie, and the red gem sparkles in the dim lighting of the club.

Motioning Rocko to set my little imp down between my legs, he does so. Ayla now stands in front of me with her back to my so-called friend. There's no way of telling who she is, especially with the drool running down her chin from the gag.

Opening my pants up, I grip the hair at her nape and ask, "Are you ready to sin with me, imp?"

Ayla's eyes light up, and she nods enthusiastically. She truly is a slut, and I don't mean that degradingly. I fucking love that she's so sexual and loves exploring everything. There's so much I'm willing to show her, but not until my revenge is complete.

So, being a sick son of a bitch once again, I push her mouth down on my cock, gagging her as I press it all the way in. The man behind her keeps his eyes on her ass the entire time.

"Look at that—she's loving it. Her cunt is dripping something fierce. Can I taste it, Beast?"

I could make it so much worse and say yes, but I will not do that to Ayla. That's some sick shit, and I don't condone incest, especially in my club.

"You touch her, Kennedy, and you will lose every one of your fucking fingers. Be a good boy and watch, and then I'll find someone to take care of you."

I don't miss the soft growl that comes from the man, but he sits back and licks his lips, continuing to watch. The reaction from Ayla isn't missed, either, but I just keep pumping her head up and down on me. Just when I'm about to come, I pull her off me.

"Kneel..."

Ayla drops to her knees, and I let go, marking her cheek, chin, and chest with my seed. When I'm finished, I tuck myself back into my pants and return to my conversation with her father.

"Have your pick of any girl here, Kennedy, and you may have her," I tell him.

He looks down at my little imp. "Are you sure I can't have her? I'll pay you a hefty sum..."

Rage burns through me. This motherfucker just doesn't give up. If Ayla weren't here, I'd teach him a lesson, but for her sake, I'll wait.

"I told you, she's *mine*. Pick someone else."

"Oh, fine. I guess a whore is a whore. Anything is better than going home to a wife who no longer puts out," he states.

"That's the spirit, old friend." I hold my glass up to salute him, pretending to be his friend again.

"How about that pretty blonde, over there? Does she like taking it up the ass?" Kennedy eyes one of the newer girls, whom I've tried, but I ended up being much too big for her.

"She's perfect for you," I answer, then motion for the sub to come over to us.

"As I said, a whore is a whore..."

"Do not call them that to their face unless you're role-playing. We respect the subs here, Kennedy—you know this."

"Yeah, yeah, yeah, I know."

I watch the two walk away toward the private rooms and then help Ayla off the floor. Removing the gag, I wipe some cum from her face and let her suck it off my finger.

"Would you like to stay, or go back to the room?" I ask her.

"Can you please take me back, Beast?" Her voice is low and whispery, and I can't help but frown.

"Are you okay, imp?"

She looks up at me, her blue eyes reminding me of a summer sky as she replies, "I just want to go back to my room. I'm feeling a bit tired, and I have work in the morning."

I study her momentarily and then nod. "Alright, let's go."

ELEVEN

Ayla

I'm sitting at my desk at work, going over everything I've learned about my father. He's stepping out on my mother, and he's being a disgusting pig about it. The fact that Beast keeps making me perform in front of my father really upsets me, but at least he has my identity hidden. I know that shouldn't matter, I should try and put a stop to it, but I doubt Beast will listen.

"Miss Kennedy, I need those files," Mr. Silverman calls out.

I jump at the sound of his voice, picking up the folder with the reports I finished just after lunch, and I hurry out of my office.

As I enter his office, I say, "I'm sorry, I—"

"Shut the door," he orders, cutting me off.

I do as he says and then walk to his desk, placing the folder in front of him. Mr. Silverman types a few things on his keyboard, then leans back in his chair, fixing his stare on me. Remaining where I stand, I keep my eyes on the folder I placed in front of him.

When nothing is said, I clear my throat, asking, "Is there anything else?"

"As a matter of fact, yes. Come here, Miss Kennedy," my boss says, pointing to the spot beside him.

My pulse races for ridiculous reasons, but I know the last time I got close, he sent me home. I need this job, though, so I do as he asks once again.

When I come to stand beside him, he then crooks his finger at me, indicating that I come closer. Bending, I close the distance as much as I can, and to my utter disbelief, Mr. Silverman grabs the back of my neck and pulls me in closer.

The sound of my boss inhaling deeply doesn't go unnoticed, but I can't do anything about it. I don't dare pull back—I need this job.

"You smell very nice today, Miss Kennedy. I'm glad you took my advice," my boss states, yet he doesn't let go.

"I'm so sorry about that. It will never happen again," I say very softly, almost whispering it.

"Never say never, Miss Kennedy..." Mr. Silverman's breath caresses my cheek as he states this in my ear.

Suddenly, I feel his tongue slide up the column of my neck, and my eyes widen. Granted, my boss is a very handsome man, but—he's my boss.

"Mm, you even taste yummy, Ayla," he growls out my name, and the sound alone has me clenching my thighs together.

"I-I'm so happy you think so," I stammer. What else do you say to your boss who's currently licking your neck?

"Do you know what else will make me happy, Ayla?" he asks, continuing to use my first name.

"W-what?" I'm not really sure I want to hear the answer.

"I want to taste more of you. Will you let me?"

"M-more, Sir?" I ask shakily.

"Yes... More. I want to know what your pussy tastes like. Would you like to come on my tongue, Miss Kennedy?"

Would I? My pussy is screaming yes, but I know Beast would never allow it. How do I say no to my boss?

"Well, I..."

"What's the matter? Does the cat have your tongue? It's either yes or no, Ayla."

"I h-have..."

What do I say? Is Beast my boyfriend? He seems too dominant to have that title. Do I tell him I have a master?

"You have what?" Mr. Silverman asks, licking my neck some more.

"I'm with someone..."

"Sorry, but I don't see anybody else here. This is my office, and what I want, I usually get." His cocky attitude reminds me of Beast, which, for some fucked up reason, really turns me on, and I whimper.

As if on cue, the phone rings, and Amilia's voice comes over the intercom when Mr. Silverman presses the button.

"Your two o'clock is on line one, Sir." Amilia's sweet voice is heard loud and clear, and I hear my boss sigh.

"Thank you, Amilia," he replies before addressing me again. "Saved by the bell. Miss Kennedy. Go grab your things and come straight back. This is an important meeting."

I nod and rush from the office, so happy to get away, even if for a moment. It's enough time to pull myself together. How the fuck did I get myself into this situation? I have to tell Beast—I can't not tell him. My primary concern is that Beast will go ape shit and kill my boss, leaving me jobless. Fuck my life...

The rest of the afternoon went without any more mishaps or inappropriate behavior from my boss. I'd be lying if I said I hated the attention because, come on, who wouldn't want to be hit on by their hot boss? However, I now have Beast, and I'm happy with him.

Beast treats me like I've always fantasized, and I'm not ashamed to admit that I love being treated as an object sometimes. It takes a lot of pressure off me to perform so perfectly. If Beast wants to use me as he sees fit to get himself off, then I'm game.

Mr. Silverman left the office right after the meeting we had with one of First Financial's biggest clients. Thankfully, he chose to leave early, which allowed me to relax before heading home myself.

Home. I can't believe I consider The Lair my home now, or more specifically, the Cave room. Smiling as I think about how Beast keeps me chained up in his *cave,* and it does things to certain parts of my body. It's fucked up, I know, but I don't care.

I'm still smiling when I greet Rocko outside as he waits to open the back door for me. When I slip into the darkened backseat, I gasp. Beast sits in the shadow on the other side of the car.

My hand flies to my chest. "Beast! You scared me!" I giggle nervously.

"I'm sorry, little imp. I thought I'd come to pick you up. I want to take you somewhere," Beast states before tapping his thigh.

Grinning, I slide over and climb onto his lap, straddling him. "Where are we going?"

"Don't worry about it. You will go where I take you. You will stay by my side and not say a word. Do you understand?"

"Yes, Beast."

He pulls me into him and begins biting my neck. I tilt my head, giving him better access as I moan, but then Beast stops abruptly.

"What is this?" he asks surly.

"What is what?" I ask, not sure what he's talking about.

It's already getting dark, so I don't know what it is he's seeing. When he turns on the overhead light and jerks my head to the side even more, I frown.

"Beast..."

"Is this a fucking hickey?" Beast's voice is dangerously low as he asks.

Fuck! Did Mr. Silverman leave a mark on me?

"I-I'm not sure what you're talking about, but I do need to talk to you about something that happened today."

"Go on..." he growls, still holding my head to the side.

Suddenly, nervousness takes hold, and now I'm second-guessing whether I should tell Beast that my boss hit on me. The silence grows as he patiently waits for me to say something.

Finally, I just blurt it out. "My boss came on to me and licked my neck..."

I'm pretty sure I stop breathing the entire time I wait for Beast's response. I expect him to blow up at this news, but instead, he asks very calmly, "Did you enjoy it?"

"What?" I jerk back, utterly confused.

"Did... You... Like... It?" Beasts asks very slowly, as if he were talking to a child.

"I couldn't tell you because I was too shocked. It didn't last long—"

"Did anything else happen?" he interrupts.

"No—I mean, he wanted to taste *other* parts, but then he was interrupted and we had a meeting, so no—nothing else happened."

Beast's hand comes up and grips my jaw. His dark eyes look black through his mask as he asks, "Who owns you?"

"You do..." I murmur through his hold.

"And who is the only one with permission to touch you?" he asks.

"You are..."

"Good girl. Anybody who touches what is mine will pay dearly," Beast informs me, lifting one brow as if waiting for me to argue, but I don't.

The car stops, and Rocko opens the door for us before Beast lets go of my jaw. Lifting and setting me beside him, Beast climbs out of the car first, then holds his hand out to help me out.

We're at some kind of warehouse, and as we walk through the massive building, I'm curious to know what all the boxes and crates hold, but I don't dare ask. I allow Beast to pull me through the building until we come to a set of doors.

"Um, can I use the restroom first?" I ask.

Beast nods. "Rocko will show you where it's at. Come straight back here. I'll be in this room here..." He points to the door right in front of us.

"Okay. I'll just be a minute," I assure Beast and hurry to catch up with Rocko.

The restroom is just around the corner, so when I exit once I'm finished and don't see Rocko waiting, I don't freak out. I follow the path back to where Beast is, but just as I round the corner, I bump into a hard wall of chest.

"Oh, I'm so sorry!" I gasp.

Large hands wrap around my biceps, ensuring that I don't fall over. However, they don't let go.

"Well, what do we have here?" A burly man stares down at me with a salacious gleam in his eye.

"I'm sorry, but I've got to go. I'm—"

"Not going anywhere, pretty girl," the man interrupts.

He pushes me against the wall, his body flattening against mine, and I can smell the sweat that's leaking through the pits of his shirt.

"Beast—"

"Oh, the boss brought us a plaything from the club again? He's such a great boss. He's got the best sluts who work for him..." The guy's hand starts to slide up my leg.

"What? No! That's not what I mean—I'm his—"

I don't get to finish my sentence as the guy is ripped away from me. A growl echoes through the hallway as Beast throws the burly man against the wall across the hall.

I watch, stunned as Beast pummels the man's face repeatedly. He stops briefly and shoves the guy so he's facing me.

"She is *mine!*" Beast states, and the man's eyes widen in horror.

A split second later, Beast is grabbing the man's head and twisting it, breaking the guy's neck in one fell swoop. I should be shocked. My pulse is racing, but not because I just watched Beast kill another person in front of me—no. I'm shocked because the whole scene now has me throbbing for the Beast.

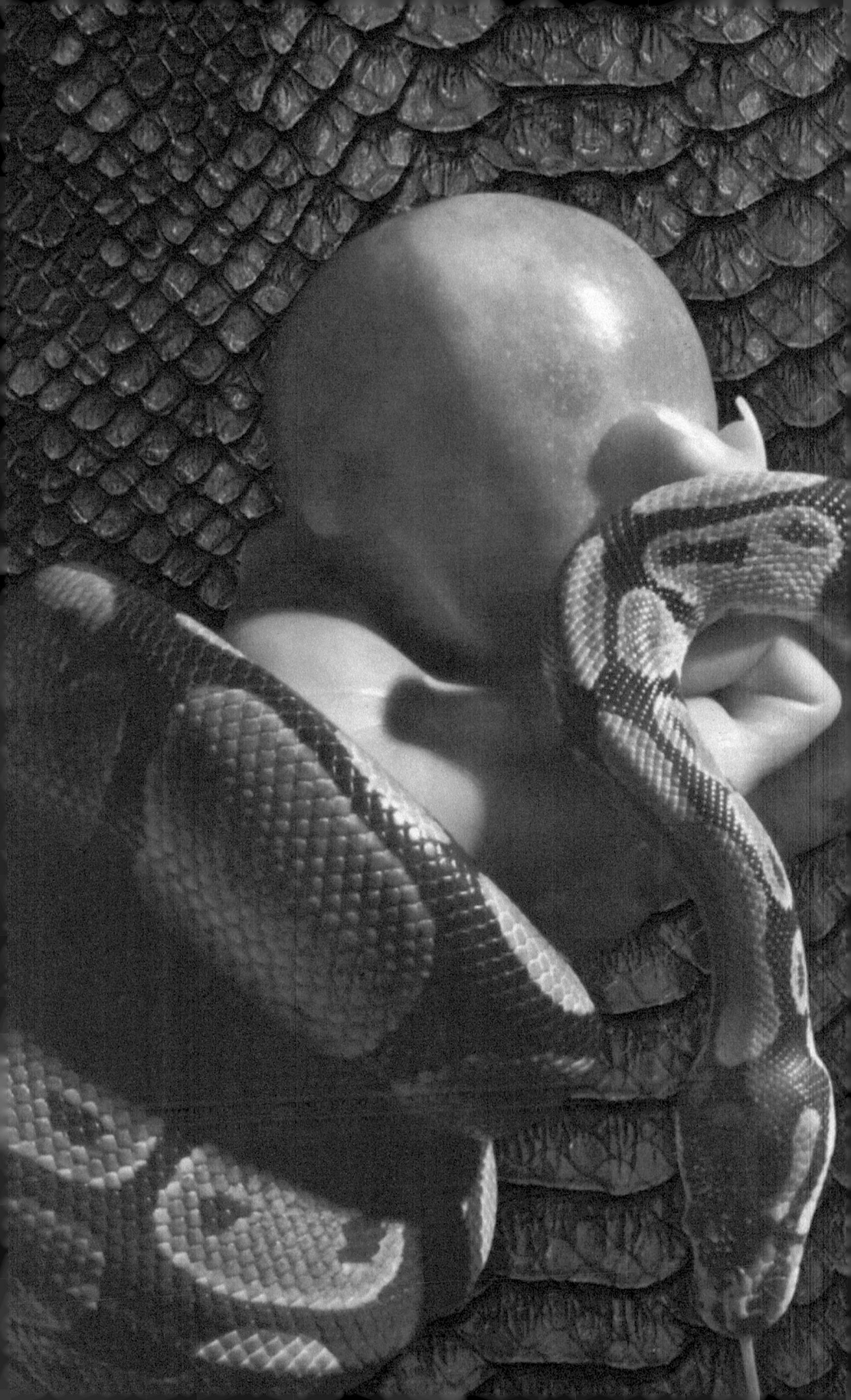

TWELVE

Beast

I should have known it was too soon to take her anywhere. I'm not in my right headspace yet. All these feelings swirling around in my head and my chest have me fucked up. The Beast doesn't catch feelings, and yet, here I am, killing anyone who dares touch my little imp.

The only thing stopping me from killing the one man that I want to bury the most is the fact that he hasn't touched her, not in a sexual way, anyway, and he never will. I wonder how he will react when he finally finds out who my pretty little whore is?

I've seen the new report from my PI, and let's just say, it isn't pretty. Dalton Kennedy has his sights on my company. He thinks he's being sneaky by trying to accomplish a hostile takeover, but we're on to him. He's now using shell corporations to buy up shares, and although my team is working on a way to prevent him from buying too many, I'm concerned it's taking too long.

That's where my slutty little imp comes into play. I heard Dalton had a daughter who was fresh out of college, looking for a job. Of course, I said yes when Dalton came to me about hiring his daughter. However, I then found her CamBaby website while searching for her online.

A plan started to formulate, and here we are. I'm not sure when I'll tell my little imp that her boss and her Beast are one and the same. I'm having way too much fun fucking with her. What started as sweet revenge has turned into more. Ayla's dark needs meet my own, and I don't think I will ever find anyone like her again.

Our age gap doesn't matter to me, not when I'm balls deep inside that gorgeous cunt of hers. It's time to step up my game and see just how dark my little imp is willing to go, and whether she'll stay or try to escape me. What she doesn't know is that no matter how many times I tell her that she can have her freedom, she will never be free of me.

I would rather lock her away in a cage like a beautiful bird and keep her for my selfish needs than to let her go on with her life without me. I'm a greedy bastard, and now that Ayla has fallen into my web, there's no getting out.

Ayla has seen me kill before, and she still allows me to take what I want. Seeing what I did to that piece of shit warehouse worker is no different. She will let me have her again and again—bet!

I'm still staring down at the motherfucker who touched my girl when another voice calls out to the corpse.

"Pete!"

I glance up just in time to see another worker shove my girl aside and drop to his knees beside his friend. I see fucking red as I watch Ayla slam into the wall and her head bounce off the smooth surface.

I grab the man by his shirt, reach into the strap at my ankle, and pull the knife I carry around out. Without hesitation, I plunge it into his gut repeatedly until finally, I wrench upwards, letting some of his intestines slip out of the gaping hole.

I let go of his shirt, allowing him to fall on top of his friend, Pete, and then I stand up. I go to Ayla, who's still standing there gawking at the two men on the floor.

"Are you okay, imp? Did he hurt you?" My gruff voice is still laced with anger from them touching what is mine.

"Beast, I..."

"Are... You... Okay?" I ask slow and growly.

"Y-yeah, I'm fine, but—"

I grip her neck and crush my lips to hers. She doesn't fight me, opening her mouth to let me in. Without releasing her lips, I walk us into the office I had just been in when I heard the commotion in the hallway.

Rocko is the only one in the room, but as soon as we enter, he slips out, closing the door behind him. *Smart man.*

Grabbing Ayla's jaw, I keep backing her up until her ass hits my desk. I shove her pencil skirt up to her waist, run the bloody blade across my pant leg, before using it to cut her panties away from her.

I bite her lip as I pull away from her, finally.

I don't say a word as I crouch down and take her into my mouth. I eat her sweet pussy like it's my last meal, and she screams each time I suck and nip at her clit. With her hands in my hair, she keeps me between her legs, grinding against my face.

"More, Beast... More!" she cries out.

Typically, I don't allow my subs to demand things from me, but I'm too lost in Ayla's essence not to give her what she's begging for. Still holding the knife, I run the tip of the handle around her wet lips while I suck on her sensitive bundle.

When my little imp moans, I push the handle up inside of her just a little. Ayla gasps and stills, but when I give her clit another hard suck, she begins to gyrate her hips. I press more of the handle into her, and soon, I'm thrusting it in and out.

I push it in until just before the blade starts and then pull it out, only to thrust it in again. Pulling my mouth off Ayla's clit, I watch as I fuck the knife handle into her, thrilled to see her enjoying it so much.

"You like being fucked with the weapon I kill with? Do you get off on me killing people for you, little imp?" I gaze up at her, and our eyes meet.

She nods.

"Words, imp. I need to hear your words."

"Yes..." she pants. "I get turned on when you kill for me, okay? Is that what you want to hear, Beast?"

I raise a brow at her tone, and then, being careful not to cut her, I flip her so she's now bent over my desk. Shoving the handle as far as I can into her heat, I tear off my belt and wrap it around her pretty little neck, tightening it until it's nice and snug.

I then open my pants, pull out my cock, and spit on her tight hole. "This will teach you to not use that tone with me, little imp."

I begin working my cock into her ass while the knife still fills her cunt. Being careful not to stab myself or her, I start rocking back and forth, pushing

81

further in a little more each time. I spit on my dick occasionally, making sure there's at least a little lube.

"Oh, God... it burns," she moans.

"Good. Perhaps it will teach you a lesson..."

As soon as I'm in completely, I reach around, take hold of the knife, and thrust it in and out. I can feel the ridges from the blade scrape against her walls, and it feels so good on my cock.

"Do you like that, little whore? You like being fucked by both a knife and my cock?" I snarl before biting down on her shoulder.

"*Agh!* Yes... Please, don't stop!"

"Not a fucking chance, imp." Biting down again, her screams are music to my ears as I feel her tighten around the knife handle and my cock as she comes.

I taste the metallic of her blood and realize that I've broken the skin. Groaning, I suck on the wound, drinking her life's essence before just licking at it until it stops dripping.

I remove the knife and shove it into her mouth. "Suck on it until I fill this ass up," I order before gripping her hips and pounding into her tight ass.

She feels too good for me to last much longer, and when I let go, I roar like the wild beast she likes so much. I collapse onto her back as I take in gulp after gulp of air. I'm pretty sure I saw spots that time.

Once I'm back in control, I pull out and tug her skirt back in place. She'll be leaking out of her ass until we get back to the club, but that's her own fault.

I reach for her, helping her to stand before I take hold of the knife and make her release it. My little imp looks dazed and thoroughly fucked, and I can't help but be proud about it. For being a forty-two-year-old guy, keeping a young, sexual woman like Ayla pleased can be a feat for some men. It's a good thing I'm not some men.

"Come, let's go home." I take Ayla's elbow and escort her out of the warehouse and back to the waiting car.

"Where is your home, Beast?" my imp asks as we settle into the backseat.

"You will find out once I know for sure that you are mine," I tell her.

"I am yours. You've told me this repeatedly."

"I have, but that doesn't make it so, now does it?"

"How am I supposed to prove to you that I am yours, Beast? I even have a tattoo on my pussy saying it's so!"

I grin wickedly at this, but still, I argue, "Something I did myself. You've never once shown me that you want to be here with me. I can't trust you not to leave at the first opportunity."

I hear her sigh from beside me, but then mutters, "It's hard to prove anything to you when you keep me locked in the cave all the time."

I turn my head to gaze at her, and when she doesn't give me her attention, I grip her chin and force her to look at me. Her piercing light eyes stare back at me with nothing but sorrow in their depths. Perhaps she's telling me the truth and does want to stay, but I still can't be sure. I need proof.

"Would you rather me treat you like my pet and keep you on a leash while I mingle within the club?"

"Would you... Really?" Her eyes light up with excitement, and my heart skips.

Ayla would rather me treat her like a fucking dog just so she could be by my side? We shall see about that. I bet she doesn't last a night.

THIRTEEN

Ayla

I'll admit that offering to be a pet for the night is a bit much, but if I have to crawl on the floor and act like a dog, I'll do it—for *him*. I don't know what's gotten into me. I've fallen down a deep, depraved hole that there's no way of crawling back out. However, I'd be lying if I said that I wanted out.

Beast has shown me the side of myself that I've always known was there. I just hadn't realized how deep my sexual urges really were. The depth of the depravity Beast bestows upon me is nothing I can't handle. But what's more, is that I find myself craving more.

Ayla Kennedy is just a name I was born into—imp is my true identity—Beast's little demon.

I take longer in the shower, making sure I clean every nook and cranny, and remove every hair that needs to be removed from my body. I then find the sheerest dress from inside my closet and put it on, leaving off my underthings. I want to show Beast that I can be his perfect little whore without him having to tell me.

When Beast arrives to escort me up to the club, excitement swims through me. However, the look he gives me when his eyes rake down my body from behind his mask tells me that he doesn't like my choice of dress.

Instead of asking me to remove it, Beast grips the neckline and tears it from my body. Without saying a word, Beast moves to the dresser on the other side of the cave and brings back a thong and a pair of pasties.

"You will wear what I want to see you in—the less clothing, the better." He smirks as he peels the backing off one of the pasties and presses it over my right nipple.

Once he adds the left pasty, he then pulls a leash from his pocket and attaches it to my collar. Not wanting him to have to tell me, I drop to my knees, and then to my hands, and wait for his praise.

I live for the Beast's praise.

Unfortunately, it doesn't come. Beast turns and heads for the door with me crawling beside him. He only stops just before opening the door to retrieve the mask he ties around my face. I don't know why he insists on still hiding my identity. I'm not ashamed to be who he needs me to be, but maybe he's ashamed of me.

I don't let that thought bother me because deep down, I don't think that's the case. Maybe one day he will tell me why, but until then, I'm happy to do his bidding and wear it.

The club is packed, and if I were with anyone other than Beast, I'd be worried about getting stepped on. Everyone makes a wide berth for the owner of The Lair, so there's no chance of me getting trampled.

Thankfully, we stop frequently, so Beast can talk to patrons. Crawling isn't for everyone—my knees are already hurting—but I won't show my discomfort.

"Beast! Long time no see," A man's voice belts out as someone steps up to us.

My head is bowed as it should be, so I can't see who it is, but I don't recognize the voice. Beast speaks with the man briefly before tugging at my leash and moving forward.

When a pair of sexy legs steps up to Beast next, a sultry voice reverberates all around us. "Oh, Beast, it's been way too long. How about you chain up your bitch, and you can have your way with me. It can be like old times."

I don't know who she's calling a bitch, but she'd better watch herself. I will not allow any hussy to put her hooks into the man that I consider mine. I memorize the black strappy heels the woman is wearing and make a mental note to look for her when I have to use the restroom. I'll make it clear that she's to stay away from Beast.

"Now, Jackie, you should know that this one is special to me. I wouldn't just chain her up while I had my fun," Beast states in an amused voice.

"Oh? What would you do then—pass her off to one of your friends?"

Laughter rumbles from Beast, and he tugs on my leash. "What do you think, imp?"

I glance up, ensuring that I don't show my true feelings, and I give him the answer that I know he wants to hear. "Whatever you wish, Master."

I don't miss the glint in his eyes as I give him the response he wants to hear. Not realizing I'm doing so, my breathing stops as I wait for what he says next.

"As much fun as it sounds—I'm going to have to pass. I only fuck my pretty little whore these days." Beast grins down at me.

My lungs inflate with much-needed air at hearing his words, and I have to bow my head to hide the smile that creeps onto my lips. I don't expect the pain that erupts in my hand as Jackie takes a step closer.

The bitch's heel is practically embedded into my hand, and yet, I don't make a sound. I believe that's precisely what Jackie was waiting for—for me to embarrass Beast by showing my weak side.

"Maybe another time, then, Beast," the woman states before stepping back, removing her heel from my hand.

Beast doesn't respond as he continues forward. It isn't until we come to a table with familiar voices that we stop again. This time, he pulls on my leash and orders me to stand. When I come to my full height, I understand why.

Sitting at the table are the same four men as that first night, including my father. His eyes are soaking me in from head to toe, and I feel bile rise in my throat.

Turning toward Beast, I ask, "May I be excused to use the restroom, Master?"

Running a thumb over my pasty-covered nipple, he grins behind his mask before he replies, "Of course, but hurry back."

"Yes, Master."

I lose myself in the crowd as I rush away, needing to get as far from that table as possible. What is Beast's game? Why does he keep doing this to me?

I push my way through the door to the women's restroom and stop short when I see a woman sitting on the chaise lounge just inside. She's rubbing her foot with one hand as she holds her black strappy shoe in the other.

Jackie smirks at me. "So, he doesn't keep you close at all times, does he? You're not as special to him as he let on."

I'm not going to let this bitch get to me, so I respond to her taunting words. "Beast is mine, and that's all you need to know. Stay the fuck away from him."

Jackie's eyes widen, and her lips curve upwards. "If he knew that you spoke to a Domme this way, he would dump your ass in a heartbeat."

Shit!

I didn't know she was a Domme—Beast will be very upset if he hears about our altercation, but at the same time, I can't allow anyone to go after what's mine.

I'm so lost in thought that I don't realize Jackie has stood up until she shoves me against the wall. She reaches over and locks the door. With her free hand, she brings it to my throat, pinning me to the wall.

"What's so special about you, hmm?" Jackie runs her eyes over my body before meeting mine again.

"Beast won't like you putting your hands on me," I mumble the best I can.

She tightens her hold on my throat. "You will not speak unless I say you can. I'm a fucking Mistress here, and I can touch any sub I choose."

"Red!" I sputter, using the universal safe word for the first time.

Jackie only laughs.

"Oh, you're funny. I only allow safe words when doing a scene. This is fucking personal. You seem to have captured the eye of the only man who can meet my needs, and I can't have that."

Suddenly, I feel something run up my thigh and realize that it's the shoe she's still holding. I grip the wrist of the hand choking me, and struggle to break free. Jackie is much stronger than I anticipated.

"Please..." I beg.

Jackie only laughs and then thrusts the heel of her shoe into my entrance. I cry out at the intrusion and try harder to get her to release me, but it seems futile.

When I start seeing black spots dance before my eyes, I stop struggling. I don't want to die this way, but I can't fight her off if I can't breathe.

"Look at that. You're such a little slut. You like this, don't you?" She pumps the heel in and out faster. "You will leave Beast alone. I don't ever want to see you here again. Otherwise, I will find bigger and sharper things to fuck this cunt with."

She doesn't know that I'm a captive here. Well, Beast at least thinks I'm a captive, but I don't ever want to leave. This is my home now.

When I nod my head, she releases my neck but keeps me pinned to the wall. I have no energy to fight her as I catch my breath. Jackie watches with amusement as she violates me, so she doesn't notice when I've finally come back to myself.

The heel is pulled from me, and Jackie holds it up in front of my face, wearing a maniacal grin as she says, "Look how wet you are. You loved it..." She then sticks the heel of her shoe into her mouth, sucking off my juices.

Something inside me snaps, and suddenly, I'm shoving the shoe into her mouth, making her take the whole six-inch heel. Blood spurts from her mouth, and I yank the heel out before stabbing it into her right eye.

The woman drops to the floor as I stand here shaking. I should be freaking out, but I'm not. Elation runs through me knowing that I never have to worry about this bitch again. Whether or not Beast will be happy is a whole other story.

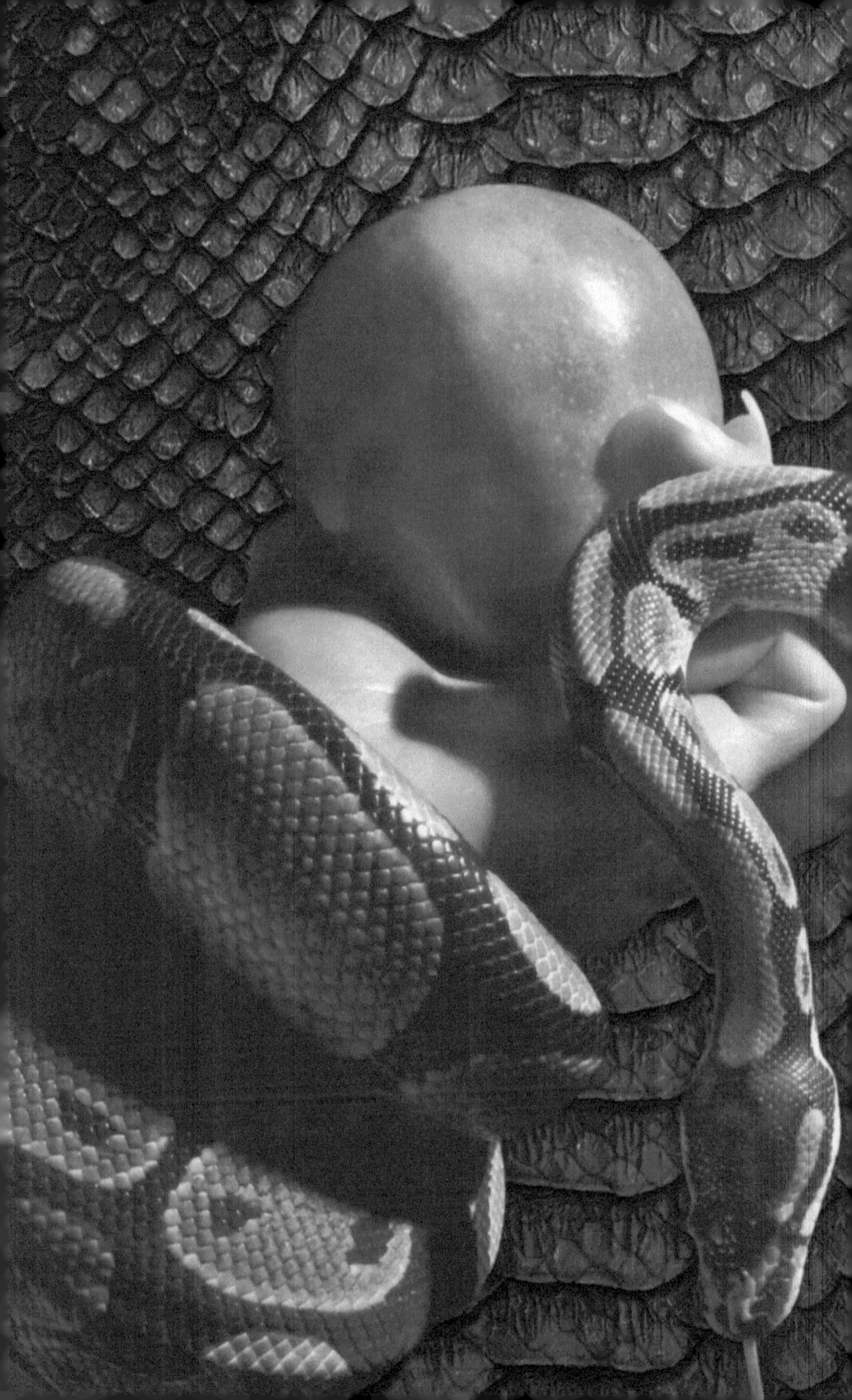

FOURTEEN

Beast

Ayla takes longer than I thought in the restroom, so I decide to go see what's keeping her. I'm glad I do. Just as I get to the women's restroom, the door swings open, and there stands my little imp.

Something about her demeanor alerts me to something being wrong, and I raise an eyebrow. Ayla looks up and down the hallway before gripping my shirt and pulling me into the restroom.

I'm about to reprimand her when I notice Jackie, one of the club's Dommes, lying on the floor with a heel protruding from her eye. I crouch down and move her onto her back, and that's when I see the blood running from her mouth, too.

"What happened here?" I don't raise my voice, but I do ask in a stern tone.

"S-she violated me with her shoe and told me to leave the club and never come back. I used a safe word, but she didn't care." Her hand absently goes to her crotch.

I watch her closely before shoving my hand between her legs and pulling her thong aside to examine her. She winces at the lightest touch, and when I pull my hand away, there's a smear of blood on my finger.

"I'm sorry that she did that to you," I tell her, standing. "I'll have someone take care of the body." I'm disturbed by what Jackie has done. I've never known her to be this aggressive.

"You're not mad at me?" Ayla asks, relief evident in her expression.

My grin should speak volumes as I direct it towards her before pulling her into my chest. "No, I'm not mad. If anything, I'm proud of you, little imp. You're living up to the name I gave you, and I'm happy to know that I'm certain I've found my other half."

Ayla pulls back a little and tilts her head so she can look up at me. "You're mine as much as I am yours, Beast. If you can kill for me, I *will* kill for you," she whispers, and I know her words to be true.

Gripping her jaw, I crash my mouth to hers, kissing them brutally. Our teeth clash together, and our saliva smears all over each other. It's a sloppy kiss, but one that will forever be burned into my memory as being the best one ever.

When we break free from the kiss, our foreheads rest against each other's as we try to control our breathing.

"How about we call it a night and go back to the cave?" I suggest lifting and throwing her petite frame over my shoulder. "I'll let your cunt heal, but I'm taking this ass." I slap the bare flesh, making her squeal in delight.

I take Ayla back to her little cave via a hidden route as I speak on the phone with the person handling the cleanup in the restroom. It doesn't take long to make it back, and I don't waste any time taking what I want from her, making my little imp surrender to my primal desires.

I enter Ayla's boss's office at First Financial before she arrives for work. It's time for this discussion to take place, and what's a better way than to do it right here?

I'm standing at the window, my arms crossed, staring out over the city, when I hear her melodic voice just outside the door. My cock stirs at the sound, and I close my eyes, enjoying the sound.

"Good morning, Mr. Silverman. I've got your coffee," Ayla says just behind me.

Using the voice I know she's come to hear every day, I reply, "Thank you, Miss Kennedy."

"Is there anything else you need at the moment?" she asks.

Grinning, I nod. "As a matter of fact, there is. Shut the door and lock it, Miss Kennedy."

"Um," she stammers a little before adding, "I don't think that's a good idea, Mr. Silverman."

"Why not?" I ask, still facing away from her.

"Well, because I have a boyfriend, and he wouldn't appreciate me being alone with you like that."

"Oh? What's he going to do to me?" I ask, hiding the amusement from dripping into my voice.

"With all due respect, Sir—he'd kill you."

I'm proud of her answer, but I'm not ready to stop this little game just yet.

"Are you a good girl for him like you are for me?" I ask.

"Mr. Silverman, I don't think this conversation is appropriate. I—"

"Answer the question, Miss Kennedy!"

My cock comes to full staff when she states, "I'm sorry, Mr. Silverman, but I can no longer work for you. Thank you for the opportunity, but I think it's best that I find another job."

I close my eyes, savoring her response. My little imp would leave her job for me. This is the best news I've heard. She's proven herself to me, and now it's time that she learns the whole truth. She needs to know why I chose her.

"I'm sorry, but I don't accept your resignation."

"You don't really have a choice," Ayla states, anger rising in her voice. "Who are you to tell me that I can't quit? I understand my father got me this job, but my father can go to hell, and if you're going to be difficult, then you can join him!"

As soon as I hear Ayla's feet shuffle and walk towards the door, I turn around and order, "On your knees, imp."

She stops short, and her body tenses as she slowly turns around. Ayla's mouth drops when she gets a look at my face, and suddenly, she's falling to her knees.

"W-what are you doing here, Beast? My boss will be here any minute—wait. Why do you sound like Mr. Silverman?"

Giving her my wickedest grin, I grip the bottom of my mask and pull it up and off my head. Ayla's gasp is loud as she takes in the sight before her.

"What's wrong, imp? You look like you've seen a ghost," I tell her.

93

"Is this some sort of game or something? What's going on?" she asks as anger replaces her surprised expression.

I stroll over to the door, shutting and locking it before turning back to the woman on her knees. "It's simple, really. Your father is trying to overtake my company. He thinks I have no idea. So, I figured that if he were going to try and take something precious to me, then I'd take something precious of his."

"Y-you used me?" Ayla sounds hurt, and even though I shouldn't care, I do.

I come to stand behind her before dropping to my knees and sliding my hands around her waist. She struggles, of course, but I hold firm.

"At first, yes," I confess. "But then I saw you and knew I needed you in my life. However, it wasn't until I had you at The Lair that I realized I would never let you go."

"You've been playing a sick game with my father! Placing me in front of him, like some whore he didn't know, got you off, didn't it?" she accuses, and I can't deny it.

"As a matter of fact, it did. Wait until Daddy finds out that he's been lusting after his own daughter. With any luck, he'll off himself and I won't have to dirty my hands with it."

"Y-you plan on killing him?" Ayla gasps again.

"You know how I feel about people touching what is mine, imp. He's trying to take my company. I can't let that slide." I let my hands come up and cup her breasts, kneading them as my mouth goes to her neck briefly. "You're mine, Ayla, and you can hate me after everything I've done, but you will never be rid of me."

I don't care what she says, Ayla isn't going anywhere. She will never find a man who can satisfy her depraved needs. I tear open her shirt and yank her bra up, releasing her bountiful breasts. I then unzip her skirt in the back before hauling her up to her feet and discarding the rest of her clothes.

My imp doesn't fight me at all.

"Go to the window, Ayla," I order.

She glances over her shoulder and gives me a slight nod before moving to the tall, floor-to-ceiling window. The way it's designed is that the glass is set at a slight angle, and when I come to stand behind her, I press her body forward, so she's flat against the glass, looking down the twenty-four stories.

I unzip my slacks and pull myself out, not wasting any time. I plunge into Ayla's heat and use her to satisfy my craving.

"Who do you belong to, imp?"

"You," she replies shakily.

"And who owns this body?"

"You do." She begins to pant as I hit deeper with each thrust.

"Who am I to you?"

"My master..."

"Good... Fucking... Girl..." I strain my voice as I slam into her cunt hard.

Luckily, the glass is reinforced for this very purpose, but Ayla doesn't know that. As I pick up my pace and fuck her harder with each thrust, I can feel her body tense. She's afraid, and yet, I'm willing to bet, very turned on. Her cunt is dripping wet.

"Tell you what, imp. We will tell your father who you are and let him live with the fact that he wanted his own daughter, and then you have nothing to do with him, or I will kill him. I'll leave it up to you."

Pressing the side of her face against the glass, I pound into her as soon as I feel my balls start pulling up. Between my treatment of her and her clit rubbing against the glass, Ayla explodes all around me, and I follow suit, filling her pussy up with every last drop.

FIFTEEN

Ayla

It's been a week since Beast, or should I say, Gunner Silverman, revealed his true self to me. I was so hurt that I didn't want to talk to him. Unfortunately, I can't stay mad at him when he fucks me the way he did. My adrenaline was pumping so hard with thoughts of that window breaking and the two of us falling to our deaths.

However, we survived and went about our day as though none of it had happened. I'm a bit relieved that I don't have to fight off my boss's sexual advances anymore, not that there were many, but still. I remember my first day of work when I laid eyes on the sexy and much older man in the elevator. Who knew that I'd be screwing him in no time?

I never took Beast to be much older than thirty, so finding out that he and Silverman were one and the same was a bit shocking. I have no complaints anymore; things have been good.

Today is Halloween, and Gunner has just informed me that we're going to a party tonight. I haven't been anywhere other than work since coming to The Lair.

"Oh?" Excitement thrums through me. "Like a costume party?"

Shrugging, Gunner's mouth tilts up on one side in the cocky little grin I've come to know as being mischievous. It doesn't give me a good vibe this time, but I'll put my trust in him. I know the beast in Gunner would never allow anything bad to happen to me—unless, of course, it is he, himself, doing the hurting.

"Something like that. I have your attire ready and waiting for you. All you have to do is shower and be ready for me when I return," Gunner states before gripping my chin and kissing me.

Licking the remnants of his kiss from my lips when he pulls away, I then ask, "Where are you going?"

"To ensure everything is ready for our arrival. That's all you need to know," Gunner replies. "You should probably take a little catnap. I plan on keeping you up until the wee hours of the morning, little imp. I want you energized for what I have planned for you."

I don't bother asking what those plans are because I know he will never tell me. So, I nod and head over to the bed and climb into it.

Gunner has taken the chain off me, making it more comfortable to sleep, but I'm still a captive in the cave. Hopefully, one day, he will trust me enough to let me go free. He should know by now that I never plan on leaving him, but I guess he needs a bit more reassurance. We'll just take it one step at a time—I can live with that—for now.

"What may I ask, is this?" I lift what looks to be a bikini made of leaves.

"That, little imp, is your costume for the festivities," Gunner replies, coming to stand behind me. He proceeds to dip his head and nibble on my neck.

"It's the end of October. Isn't it a bit chilly to wear such a costume—and who exactly am I going to be?" I ask, dropping the foliage onto the bed and tilting my head to the side to give him better access.

"The theme of the party is famous historical couples. You, my little pet, will be going as Eve." Gunner's mouth latches back onto my neck.

"And will you be going as Adam, or the snake. After all, the snake is the one who tempted Eve..."

A deep chuckle rumbles against my skin, and Gunner lifts his head. "If we're being technical, the scholars say that Adam and Eve aren't a real historical couple."

"Oh? What are they then?" I turn my head, stretching my neck to stare my beast in the eye.

"It's said that it's a myth, crafted to convey a narrative. It's said to explain the origin of sin. Suffering and death then follow, and a bunch of other gibberish that I don't want to get into. All you need to know is that you are the embodiment of sin; therefore, you are Eve."

"Well, you never answered my question. Which one are you going as—Adam or the snake?"

"You will find out once we get there. The submissives come dressed, and their Doms will change once we get there," Gunner explains.

"Oh, so we freeze our asses off while you stay toasty warm?" I scoff, turning my head when he tries to kiss me.

He grips my chin, forcing my head back the other way. "I will keep you warm. Make no mistake, little imp." Releasing my chin, he steps away. "Get dressed—Rocko is waiting with the car."

Narrowing my eyes at him, I then snatch up the foliage and go to the bathroom, where I put it on. I have to admit, it's stunning on me. A little revealing, but it's not like others haven't seen most of my goods before.

When I exit the bathroom, Gunner grins, running his tongue across his lips as he slowly approaches. He slips an arm cuff on my bicep, and I notice it's a gold snake with rubies as eyes—it's stunning.

I'm pulled against my beast's broad chest before he grips the hair at the nape of my neck and gives it a tug. It's none too gentle, and I feel the tingles start at my core.

"I'm going to fuck you in the car, and fill you up with my seed. I want to make sure everyone at the party knows that you are off limits. If anyone touches you, they will not be leaving that party, except in a body bag." Gunner's kiss is unforgiving as he claims my mouth.

Wrong or not, warmth spreads through me from his declaration. I am all kinds of shades fucked up to be swooning over someone willing to kill for me. Not just willing, but has killed for me—that is fucked up, right?

My beast made good on his words and had me bend over the seat in the limo while he fucked me. I swear, he had the whole car rocking as Rocko drove us the twenty minutes to our destination.

THE SINNER IN ME

The flimsy thong holding the leaf in front of my crotch did nothing to contain the thick fluid dripping out of me. My thighs shine with Gunner's seed, and he grins as we walk inside a stunning mansion.

The party is already in full swing when we enter. Gunner walks me to a room where there are refreshments and tells me that he will return shortly. I assume he's going to change, since he's the only one not in costume at the present time.

I notice that all the submissives are barely wearing a stitch, and none of them wear a mask. I was surprised when Gunner informed me that I no longer needed to wear a mask. He said that if I'm going to be with him, then I should not be ashamed of what he does to me in the presence of others—and I'm not. Well, aside from my father's presence.

Grabbing a drink from one of the servers, I stand here and take in the partygoers. They all look like they're enjoying themselves—even the submissives aren't being contained to their usual positions by their Doms' sides. They're dancing and laughing with other subs, and a smile grows on my lips at the sight.

"I didn't know I raised such a fucking whore. Your mother would be so ashamed!" a voice behind me sneers.

I don't have to turn around to know who it is. My whole body tenses momentarily, but then I think about his words, and anger rises. I spin around and face my father.

"Oh? I would disappoint her? How about you, Father? Does Mom know that you go to sex clubs and fuck women half your age?"

My father steps closer and lowers his voice to a low, menacing tone as he grips my arm. "You don't know what the fuck you're talking about. If you dare say anything to your mother—"

"You'll what?" An angry Gunner towers over my father from behind.

I look over at my beast, and my breath catches. Gunner stands there, in all his muscular glory, wearing nothing but a loincloth. Ridges of muscle ripple across his chest and abs, sculpting him into a Greek god brought to life. I will never get over the sight of this beautiful and powerful man standing before me.

My father drops his hand and straightens before spinning on Gunner. "How dare you flaunt my daughter the way you've been doing? You... You..." my father stammers.

"I what? Fucked your daughter while you watched, drooling like a sick fool. Made her suck my cock while you begged to have her afterwards? Did you forget that it was *you* who was salivating over your daughter's cunt as she was bent over, and that it was *you* who begged to pay me to let you have her for a night?"

Listening to Gunner name off all the times my own father lusted after me makes me want to vomit. I don't care if he didn't know it was me... It's still disgusting. The fact that he would fuck someone his daughter's age isn't much different.

"I thought we were friends, Silverman? Had I known you would turn my baby girl into your whore, I never would have suggested you hire her," my father snarls.

"No. You just wanted to get your daughter in the door, so when you did the hostile takeover, she would already know how to run my business," Gunner drawls. "Do you honestly believe that I wouldn't find out what you were doing?"

"What? You have no proof—"

"Don't I?" Gunner cocks a brow as he cuts my father's words off. "Not only am I going to keep my company, but I now have my perfect little whore."

I move to stand by Gunner's side, which only makes my father's eyes bulge in disbelief. He looks back and forth between me and my beast before narrowing his eyes on me.

"Do you hear that, Ayla? He has no respect for you—you're nothing but his whore!" My father's face is as red as a tomato, but all I can do is smile.

I drop to my knees and wrap my arm around Gunner's thigh. "No, Father. I'm his *perfect* little whore, and his submissive. This is what I was born for. Gunner is precisely what the sinner in me needs."

My father's hand goes up into the air, but before he can bring it down on me, Gunner grabs his wrist, growling, "Do it and lose it." There's a staring match, which my father loses. Gunner releases his wrist and shoves him back. "Now, I suggest you get the fuck out of here before I make an example out of you."

I don't have to guess what Gunner means by *example*, and I'm glad he's at least giving my father a chance. I hate to admit it, but I don't think I would have.

My father glares at me briefly while holding his wrist, and then he's gone. It isn't until he's no longer standing in front of me that I notice the audience we attracted. I feel horrible, but Gunner doesn't seem bothered by it.

Holding out his hand, he helps me to stand. "Come, there are a few friends that I want you to meet before the main attraction begins."

I nod and follow my beast out of the room, not leaving his side until I have no choice. It's when Gunner informs me that I must ready myself with the other submissives.

"Ready myself for what, exactly?" I eye him suspiciously.

The wicked grin that I've grown to love spreads across his face. His eyes peruse me from head to toes before landing on my eyes once again. "Ready for *The Hunt*."

SIXTEEN

Ayla

I wasn't sure what to expect when Gunner mentioned The Hunt. Thinking it was like a scavenger hunt or even an Easter egg hunt, you can imagine my surprise when it was neither.

All the submissives were asked to line up by a door at the back of the mansion. We were then given a five-minute head start before being ordered outside.

The grounds at the back of the estate have been turned into a haunted maze that stretches out to God knows where. I can see woods in the distance, set at the back of the property, but aside from that, everything else is unknown.

In nothing but our costumes, all the submissives, including myself, set off in all different directions. The rules are that if our Dom finds us, within a two-hour time frame, they can do whatever they want with us. If we can hide and refrain from being caught, the roles switch, and we can dominate our Dom for the rest of the night.

This isn't a game for the faint of heart. There's depravity to be had, yet it's all in good fun. At least for those of us who crave it, and I'm all for it. To be able to stay hidden from the Beast just to watch him crawl at my side later is all the incentive I need as I take off, sprinting through the maze.

Unfortunately, as I get deeper into the maze, I realize that there isn't a spot to hide. There is nothing but walls all around us. I must reach the end of the maze and pray that there are more options.

My heart races as I continue to run, and a thrill of excitement runs through me at the fear of being caught. It's not that I'm afraid to have Gunner catch me, but I really want to be able to make him submit to me for once, just to see how it feels to have that kind of power. The power of knowing what it feels like to have someone gift you all their trust.

Squeals and giggles float through the air, telling me that our time is up and our Dom is coming for us. Some are already being caught, which leads me to believe they weren't trying very hard.

There's something up ahead, so I push myself harder. Smiling, I run toward the exit. I don't stop once I pass through the opening, even though the massive corn field is startling to see.

Diving between the stalks, I don't stop. However, it does slow me down. I'm unsure if I'm still on the right path or if I've deviated from it. My hope is to reach the woods, where I'm sure I can find a hiding place.

A sound from my right prompts me to push forward. I don't know if it's another submissive or one of the Dominants, and I'm not that girl who slows down to look and see who or what is there. It's bad enough that I broke my rule of entering a damn corn field, but what other choice did I have?

It's dark, and the only light I have is the sliver that the moon is giving me, and that isn't much at all. All I keep thinking is that I have to be getting closer to the other side.

When I come to a slight opening, I get excited until I see the large wooden beam with a scarecrow tied to it. So, I continue as I cross the opening and re-enter the corn field.

I never hear their approach, but suddenly, I'm grabbed from behind, and a hand covers my mouth. Just when I think Gunner has found me, I hear the whispered words in my ear, and I freeze.

"Did you honestly think that you could whore yourself out and flaunt what your mother and I gave you without any consequences?"

I begin to struggle.

My father only laughs as we fall to the ground with me face down in the soil. His hand is removed, but my father shoves a handkerchief into my mouth and captures my hands behind my back.

"I don't know who you think you are, but you're not my sweet, Ayla. The costume is very fitting for you, *Eve*. You're just like the Bible warns us

106

about—you're a temptress. You've tasted the forbidden fruit, and now you're tempting your own father!"

I continue to fight, trying to get him to release his grip, but he's stronger than I thought. Hot tears stream down my face—tears of sadness, fear, and most of all, anger.

My father grips my hair and pulls back, causing my body to arch in an uncomfortable position. His hot breath blows across my face, and I squeeze my eyes shut.

"Daddy Dearest is going to teach his little Eve what happens when you flaunt the forbidden fruit in front of him." He slams my face into the ground, and I see stars dance across my vision, but then I hear it. The distinct sound of a zipper. Horrified by what he's about to actually do, I try bucking up and down.

I don't stop, even when he brings his hand down hard on my bare ass cheek. The thong bottoms I'm wearing don't do anything to cover any of my ass, and will allow him much easier access, but I'll be damned if I let him do it without a fight.

Just when I start running out of steam, a crazed roar echoes all around us, and then I'm freed. I scramble around, turning to see what's happening, and that's when I see Gunner. He has my father by the shirt and is holding him in the air.

Pulling the handkerchief from my mouth, I spot my father's pocket knife that he always carries in his pants pocket. Picking it up, I run to him, still seeing red as I stab him in the torso.

Gunner drops him onto the ground, and I stab my father a few more times. It's just a small pocket knife, so I'm not sure how much damage it's really doing. After about ten stab wounds, I'm grabbed from behind and pulled away from my father. I'm still focused on hurting him that I accidentally plunge the knife into Gunner's shoulder.

I gasp.

Gunner stares at the knife embedded in his shoulder, then at me, and grins. "Do you feel better, little imp?" he asks, plucking the blade from his flesh as if it were just a tiny thorn.

"Oh, my God! I'm so sorry! I didn't mean—"

Gunner grabs my face between his hands, cutting me off. "Shh, it's okay. You're okay—he can't hurt you anymore." He pulls me into his arms and kisses my head.

I jump at the sound of a groan, and then a grunt. Pulling away from Gunner, I turn to see my father trying to crawl away. I start for him, but Gunner stops me.

"Let me finish this..."

There's a thick piece of wood on the ground, which Gunner picks up as he walks over to my father. He brings it down on my father's head again and again. I never take my eyes off the scene as the man I love bludgeons my father to death. A feeling of relief floods me, and I thank God that I have Gunner.

I've never known my father to be this sort of man. He may have been stern when it came to responsibilities, but he's always loved me, and I'm not talking about the sick kind of love. I have no idea what came over my father to turn him into a disgusting pig of a man, but I don't regret what we're doing now. If anything, we may be stopping him from doing this to others.

I stare in complete awe as Beast beats my father until he's no longer recognizable. Only when I'm certain my father is dead do I go to Gunner and wrap my arms around his waist.

"He's gone, Baby. You killed him—he's dead," I state matter-of-factly.

Gunner drops the bloody piece of wood with pieces of my father's skull and brain matter coating it in places, and turns to me. We stand here in each other's arms for a few minutes, until Gunner reluctantly pulls away.

"Come on. We need to turn this into a lesson before we get rid of the body," Gunner states, grabbing my father's leg and dragging him back through the cornfield.

Beast/Gunner

After grabbing the ladder from the shed, not too far from the center of the cornfield, I made my way back to where I left Ayla. The relief on her face when I returned didn't help with all the emotions I was already feeling.

Coming up on the scene of Ayla's father about to rape her, I saw fucking red. I've never known anyone who could be as sick as Kennedy was—who would do that to their own child.

I won't lie. Ayla stunned me when she stabbed her father. I was about to pull his limbs from his body, one by one, but she stopped me. Watching my little imp take back control like that was such a turn-on. The way she kept bringing the knife down repeatedly had me getting fucking hard.

It felt good snuffing out the bastard's last breath as I beat him over the head. He should have known better than to touch what was mine. Had I not placed the tracker on Ayla's costume, I don't know what would have happened. Yeah, the Dominants cheated and tracked our subs, so sue us. There's no way we will ever let our submissives have that kind of power over us. They'd have way too much fun.

My question is, how the fuck did her father find her before me?

"You're so wrong, do you know that?" my little imp asks, grinning.

"Yeah, but you love it." I yank her to me and crash my lips to hers.

The sound of footsteps approaching has me looking towards the front of the field. Faces come into view, and then someone asks, "What the fuck is that?"

Ayla and I glance in the direction where one of the Dominants is pointing, and I turn back to the now-growing crowd. I stare at each of them until they go silent and I have everyone's attention.

"Be warned!" I point at the corpse of Ayla's father now hanging in the scarecrow's place up on the wooden beams. "*This* is what will happen to anyone who touches what is mine..." Cupping my hand around Ayla's neck, I tug her into my chest, so everyone can get a good look at her as I finish saying, "And this gorgeous creature is *mine*!"

My friend, Drako, makes his way to the front, whistling. "Damn, Beast. That fucker still owed me money from our last card game."

"I'll cover his debt. Don't fucking worry about it." I look at the crowd and ask, "Do any of you have an issue with this?"

They all shake their heads.

"Good. Now, get the hell out of here so I can fuck my girl!"

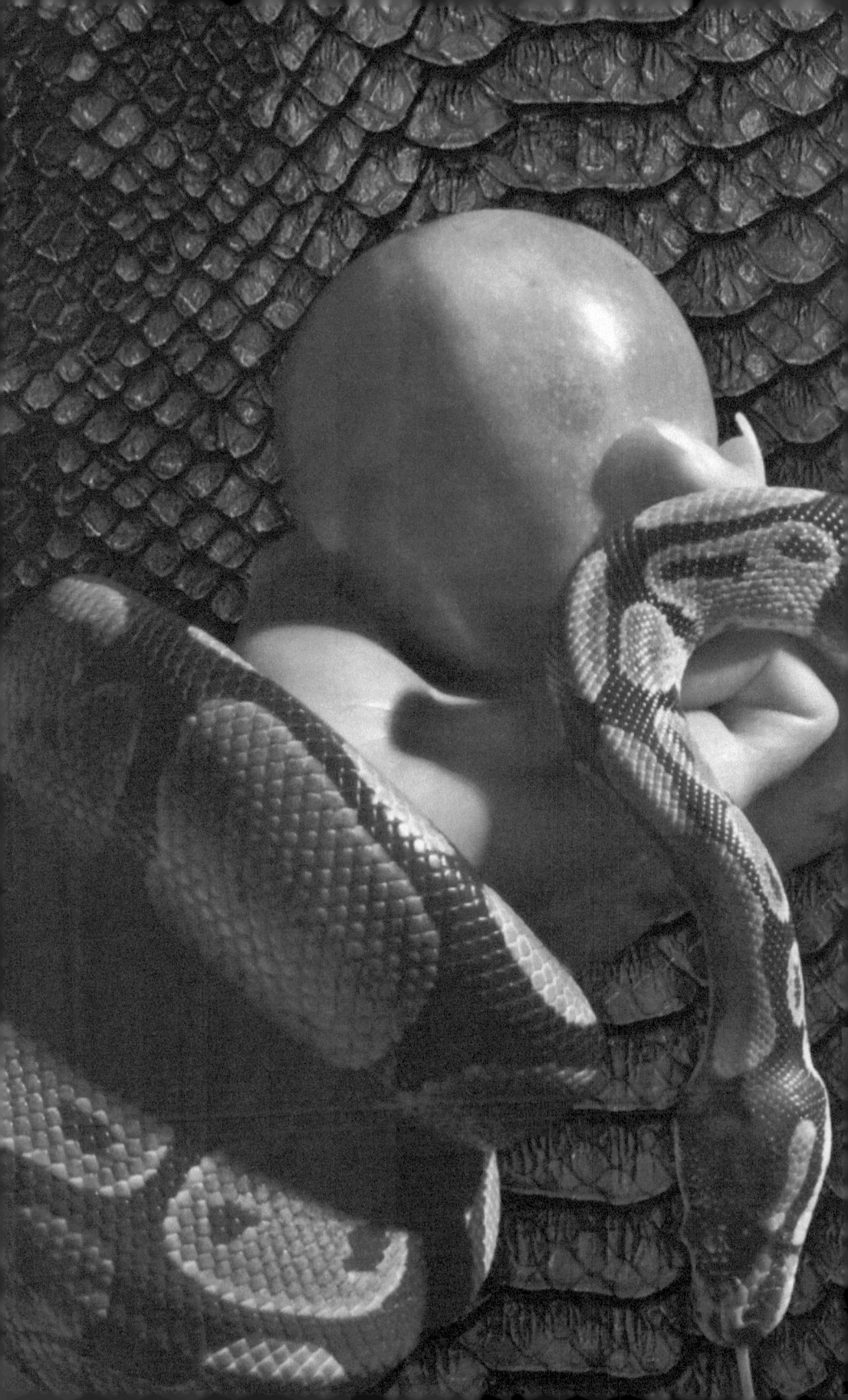

SEVENTEEN

Beast

"That's it... Take it all, little imp. I'm so proud of you," I tell Ayla as I have her on her back with my cock shoved deep inside her ass.

I'm working the fat corn cobb with a rubber on it into her greedy little cunt. Knowing I would find her, I waited until I knew she was in the field before coming after her. I had shoved one of my gold-foiled packages into my loincloth when I changed into my costume because even I couldn't be that much of a prick. I picked the fattest and longest cobb I could find as I made my way to her.

"Beast..." my little imp says breathlessly. "It's too much."

"You can take it," I tell her.

"Not with you in my ass!"

"Yes—you can, and you will. Would you rather I fist you?" I tease.

"Oh fuck..." she breathes as her wetness seeps out.

"I think you like that idea. This pretty little cunt is weeping for it. Maybe another time. Right now, you're going to fuck this corn cobb I brought for you."

I pull the cobb out to the tip and spit down on it, providing a little more lubrication before pressing it back in. I work it in slowly—not just for Ayla's benefit, but also for mine. The dried-up corn causes a nice ribbing action that I can feel as I thrust it in and out of my girl.

When I finally get the whole length into her, I leave it in for a few moments while I pound into her ass. I rub her clit as I do so, making her come all over the cobb.

"That's my dirty little whore. Lube that up nice and good." I watch her take both girths, and it almost has me losing it.

"Fuck, I'm so full, holy shit!" she cries out as I thrust into her while pulling the cobb out.

"Oh, fuck me, imp!" I clench my teeth.

The way her walls grip my cock as she comes has me following suit, filling her ass up full. She should have plenty of lubricant now.

"Just wait until my little friend here fucks this gorgeous ass," I tell her.

"Wait-what?" she pants, but I ignore her.

Pulling out of her, I flip her onto her hands and knees, ordering, "Head down, ass up, little imp."

"Beast..."

"Ass up, head down... Now!" I demand, and she obeys. "Good fucking girl.

I remove the cobb from her cunt and work it into her ass. Kneeling behind her, I bury my face in her sopping pussy as I fuck the cobb up her ass. My girl is so fucking hot when she lets me fuck her with whatever I want. I'm going to have to get creative—see how freaky she really is.

"Come for me, Ayla," I murmur against her pussy lips before motorboating the fuck out of them.

Blowing out, I thrash my head back and forth, causing the vibration through her lips, and in seconds, I have her coming all over my face. I don't stop there. I make my little imp come three more times before I decide it's getting too cold for her to be outside.

It's dark as we make our way back to the mansion, and not wanting her to hurt herself, I carry an exhausted Ayla all the way back. By the time we make it back, my little imp is sound asleep. Instead of returning to the party, I take Ayla to the bedroom upstairs and tuck her in for the night.

I step out of the open stall shower and wrap a towel around my waist before walking out into the master suite. My little imp still lies sound asleep on the plush California King; her breathing is soft and steady. A slow curve tugs at my lips as I recall the way I wore her out, fucking her into exhaustion.

I walk to her side of the bed, gazing down at her beauty. I don't know what she's doing to me, but I'm kind of liking it. Who knew that I would fall in love with someone, never mind a woman who has the same depraved kinks that I have? Ayla may be young, but she's more mature than most women my age.

Lifting my hand, I gently sweep a strand of hair from her face. Even though it's gentle, it still stirs her, lashes fluttering as her eyes slowly open. Her smile is soft and mesmerizing, causing the towel to rise, giving away the effect she has on me.

"Mm, good morning," she says, sleepily.

"Morning. Are you hungry?" I ask.

Ayla's eyes move downward, lighting up when she spies the tented towel. She licks her lips and grabs for the fabric at my waist.

"I'm ravenous..."

Chuckling, I grip her wrist and push it above her head before yanking the covers down. She's still in her costume from last night, and it takes little effort to rip it off her when I hook my fingers over the string between her breasts and pull.

"I wasn't talking about having me, although I'm not opposed to it. But you need real food."

She sticks her bottom lip out in the cutest pout. "You're such a tease."

"Good God, I've created a monster," I say mockingly before bending over and nipping her nipple.

"Mm, do we have time, or will the owner be expecting us to vacate the room?" she asks as she arches her back, offering her breast to me.

Releasing her nipple, I say, "I'm sure we can have you placate him if he does."

Ayla gasps and tries to tug her hand from my grip. "I will not have sex with anyone but you, Gunner!"

"Well, I guess it's a good thing that I'm the owner of the estate then, isn't it?"

"Huh? This is your house?" The shock on her face is priceless.

"No." I shake my head. "It's *our* house."

"Ours?" She's beginning to sound like a parrot now.

"Yes," I say, chuckling. "I've already had most of your things moved in. There are a few items I've put in storage for you to go through, but most of your belongings from your apartment are already here."

"Since when?"

Shrugging, I nonchalantly say, "Going on two weeks now?"

"You've kept me in that room at the club when I could have been staying here, with you?"

"I wanted to tell you who I was before moving you in with me, just in case you rejected me," I tell her.

"So what? Had I rejected you, you would have released me?"

I throw my head back, laughing. "Of course, not. You would have stayed in the Cave until you were ready to forgive me. You were mine the moment my eyes fell on you, Ayla."

"Please, release my wrist, Gunner."

I linger for a moment, eyes locked on hers, before finally pulling my hand away. The instant I do, Ayla sits up and slips her arms around my neck. I'm usually the one who initiates the kiss, but when my little imp forgets herself and takes the lead, I can't help but grin—and give her anything her little heart desires. I'll dole out her punishment later...

Ayla walks into my office the following workday, iPad in hand, ready to take notes for the video conference about to take place. She wears a snug pencil skirt with a silk blouse that may or may not have one too many buttons undone. My little imp loves to tease me when we're at work.

Amelia has been informed of our relationship and very much approves of it. She's been with me for years and has seen how surly I can be, but since Ayla joined our team, my attitude has severely changed, and my receptionist loves the new change.

I direct Ayla to the couch in the corner of my office and motion for her to lift her skirt. With a slight smirk, my imp hikes up her skirt and sits down. The little minx isn't wearing any panties.

My cock hardens instantly.

The video conference starts, and I see my client on the other end, smiling. "Mr. Silverman, I'm so happy you could work me in last minute," Johnson states.

"Of course. I just so happened to have had another appointment cancel on me this morning," I tell him.

While talking with my client about numbers, Ayla is taking notes, but when our eyes meet, her perfectly sculpted brow rises. I place two fingers on my desk and spread them. She knows exactly what I'm telling her to do, and like a good girl, she opens her beautiful thighs.

My beautiful pussy stares back at me, causing me to lick my lips before replying to Johnson. Turning my hand, I wiggle my middle finger, and I watch as my little imp pushes two of her fingers into herself and starts fucking them, all while typing on the tablet with her other hand. My girl is a woman of *many* talents.

I know the moment Ayla is about to come, and I wag my finger back and forth, earning me a glare from those seductive blue eyes. I'm ready to burst myself, so I wrap up the meeting and end it before pushing my chair back.

"Get that slutty little cunt over here, so I can punish it," I growl.

Ayla wastes no time rushing over to me and bending over my desk. She's fucking soaked, and I can't help but run my tongue over the glistening folds just to get a taste of her.

I slap her ass hard once I've done so before standing and releasing my raging dick from its confines. Reaching over, I grip her hair and pull her head back.

"You're such a dirty little imp, fucking yourself in front of your boss. Do you think I'd let you get away with leaving this office without me destroying this gorgeous cunt?"

"Please, Gunner..." Ayla pants, so ready to be fucked senseless.

"I'll let you have your way for now, but when we get home, you will receive your punishment. Don't think I'll let it slide, having you tease me by not wearing panties. I believe you've broken one of the dress code rules, Miss Kennedy."

"Mm, yes, Mr. Silverman. But don't forget, we must stop at my mother's first to talk to her about my father," she reminds me.

Ah yes. I almost forgot. Mrs. Kennedy has been blowing up Ayla's phone, which I finally gave back to her, because her husband hasn't come home. Telling someone that their husband will never come home isn't something that can be said over the phone, so we decided to stop by today.

I sincerely hope the woman doesn't give us any issues. Otherwise, I'm not opposed to taking care of her as well. Nobody will prevent me from being with my little imp.

Gripping her hips, I pound into Ayla from behind, not letting up until she's screaming my name. I already plan on having this time with my imp be a daily occurrence, so Amelia may as well get used to it.

Ayla's cunt squeezes the life out of my cock, causing me to follow right behind her. Our coupling is nothing less than explosive every time we're together, and I don't plan on ever giving it up.

The captive has now become the captor as Ayla secures her own collar around my once cold heart. As I spill the last of my seed into her, I confess the one thing I never thought I would.

"I fucking love you, Ayla Kennedy..."

EPILOGUE

Ayla

"Mom, are you okay?" I ask as she just stands there with her arms crossed over her chest, staring out the window.

My mother turns her head slowly and gives me a sad smile. "I will be. I'm so sorry you had to go through that, Ayla. I've known for a long time that your father was stepping out on me. At first, I tried so hard to keep his attention, but after so long, I decided that it wasn't worth catching anything from all the women he was sleeping with."

"Oh, Mom!" I go to her and wrap my arms around her.

"I'm going to be okay. You did what you had to do. I never thought he would try anything like that." My mother gives her attention to Gunner, who's standing silently by the door. "Thank you for protecting my daughter."

He nods. "I will always protect Ayla, Mrs. Kennedy."

That was nine months ago. Having to tell my mother how her husband was unfaithful, not only with other women, but that he also tried to be with her daughter, was not a conversation that I would wish upon anyone. Thankfully, my mother took it better than I expected and ended up keeping our secret. She even went to the police department to report my father as a missing person.

Gunner and his team have been working hard to keep them from finding our doorstep. The partygoers are all hush-hush about it, especially after they found out who I was to the deceased.

My father's body washed up on shore a month ago, and although his death was ruled a homicide, it's rumored that he owed money to the wrong people, and they're the ones being investigated.

I'm finally resting a little easier these days. After all, I'm not used to killing people, not like my beast is, so I've spent all this time worrying about being hauled off to jail. Now that it seems to be past us, I can finally focus on my future with Gunner—the love of my life.

We've professed our love to each other and have spent every day since showing the other just how much. We're either making love in our bed, fucking at the office, or role-playing at The Lair. Either way, Gunner is always inside of me every chance he gets.

"Mm, there you are, little imp. I've been looking all over for you," Gunner hums as he walks into the small playroom we have at home.

It's our first anniversary, and I want to make it one he will never forget. I'm bent over the padded table with my legs spread and my ankles secured, while my wrists are cuffed together over my head.

"I've been here waiting for you, Master."

"Oh? What exactly have you been waiting for me to do, little imp?" Gunner circles the table, ensuring I'm secured while running his fingers over my skin. Goosebumps rise, spreading across my flesh as he does so.

"Whatever you wish, Master. No safe word tonight." I bite my lower lip as my core begins to throb at just the thought of the kind of torture he might inflict upon me.

"Are you sure you want to go that route?" he asks, cautiously.

"Yes, Master. Do with me as you please."

"I have waited for this day ever since I brought you into my life, little imp. I'm not going to pass up the chance to see what this beautiful body can really take." The way Gunner says this is creepy, but instead of becoming worried, it turns me on.

The first thing Gunner does is insert an open-mouthed gag so I can't speak, yet I can still take his cock if it's his wish.

"I want to see you be a drooling fucking mess when I destroy this cunt." He slaps me between the legs, making me jerk.

My eyes roll back from the stinging sensation it creates, and I wiggle my ass for more. However, Gunner only giggles and ignores me as he gets to work repositioning me to his liking.

Now lying on my back with my hands above my head, Gunner straps each of my thighs and pushes them back before securing them in place. My thighs now rest against my chest while my pussy is on display for him.

"Look at that. You've got such a pretty pussy, Ayla. I can just imagine what it would look like all stretched out. Oh, wait—I'm about to find out."

I try moaning his name, but everything I say is jumbled because of the gag. Drool runs down the side of my face, and Gunner bends over, dragging his tongue up its path before spitting it out between my legs.

"You're going to need all the lube you can get for this, little imp."

He's not going to do what I think he's going to do... Is he?

My beast leaves me to retrieve something and returns with a bottle of lube. I jerk when the cool gel squirts onto my clit and folds, but then I moan as Gunner begins to rub it around my entrance.

When I feel him add more to my ass, I whimper. It's not that I'm scared for him to fuck that hole—I whimper because he's not doing it fast enough. The long moan that I let loose as soon as he slides all the way in doesn't go unnoticed.

"My girl loves her ass fucked don't you?"

I nod.

"Maybe we should let your viewers watch what I'm about to do. Would you like me to turn on the camera?" Gunner grins wickedly, and I quickly nod my head.

I don't do cam work very often anymore, but when I do, it's because Gunner wants to show off to all my viewers that I'm his and that they will never have me. I don't mind—I love being owned by the Beast. The sinner in me cannot get enough of what Beast has to offer.

Gunner leaves me long enough to set up the camera and ensure that my face isn't showing before he thrusts back into my ass.

"Fuck, CamBaby, your ass is so fucking tight!" His fingers go back to thrusting inside of me, only this time, he's added another digit.

One by one, he adds a finger until he's got all four fucking me. Adding more lube, Gunner slowly pushes his thumb into me. I groan as my head lolls to the side.

"Does that hurt?" he asks.

I shake my head. I want to tell him I want more, but the gag prevents me from doing so. The way he has me restrained, I can't move at all.

With every little thrust, I feel my pussy being stretched more and more. I glance at him, and the smile that's spread across his face is one of amazement and a bit of mischievousness.

His eyes meet mine, and he nods. "We're doing this, and you're going to take it all."

My eyes roll back when I feel more pressure and realize his knuckles have passed through my opening. He's doing it—he's going to fist me while fucking my ass!

My head begins to thrash some more when I feel more stretching as he closes his hand inside of me. Gunner proceeds to pump his fist in and out, hitting my G-spot repeatedly.

The overwhelming feeling of needing to pee takes over, and suddenly, I'm spraying out all over Gunner. He continues to fuck me with both fist and his cock, too enthralled with the fact that he's got me spread so wide.

Gunner is no longer paying attention to me as he chases after his own relief, so he doesn't notice when I begin choking on the built-up saliva pooling in my mouth. Without any way of informing him, my only chance is if he looks at me.

Tossing his head back, Gunner closes his eyes as he fucks me even harder. The jerking of my body does nothing to stop me from choking. If anything, it's making it worse. Black dots dance in front of my eyes as my lungs begin to burn.

I'm unable to get any oxygen as my saliva continues to accumulate. Every time I try breathing through my nose, I start to choke. I tilt my head, but I can't get it all to drip out. I'm fading fast, yet my body deceives me by coming again and again.

The last thing I remember is Gunner snarling as he continues to thrust into me. The sound is primal and animalistic—and it's the most beautiful thing that I've ever heard. Unfortunately, it's the last thing I ever hear.

Beast/Gunner

We've talked about fisting in the past, but I never thought I'd get the chance to do it with my little imp. I was perfectly fine with not doing so, but I couldn't pass up this chance.

She looks so beautiful the way I have her trussed up for me—she's wide open for the taking. As I slide my hand the rest of the way into her well-lubed pussy, my cock twitches in anticipation. Her walls stretch beautifully around my hand as it disappears inside of her.

I'm pretty sure the tips of my fingers are touching areas it has no business touching. I glance at the woman who has all of my heart and ensure she isn't in any pain. When I know for sure it's a green light, I start to close my hand one finger at a time. Once my fist is formed, I grin and start pumping into her. It's mesmerizing watching her take my fist and wrist, especially with my girthy cock still in her ass.

Ayla was made for me, and I will never let her go—she owns all of me. I lose myself every time I'm inside of her, and this time is no different.

Fisting my imp for the first time, I make her squirt, but I don't stop there. I want—no, I need—more from her.

Dropping my head back, I close my eyes and let myself *feel* the unimaginable euphoric sensation that washes over me. I've dominated plenty of women, but never anyone like my Ayla—nobody compares to my little imp.

I pull a few more orgasms from her body as I continue to fuck her. My climax is just on the horizon. I glance down, wishing I could see eyes when I fill her.

"Look at me, Ayla. Watch me give you everything I have."

She ignores me, but her head moves from side to side. I feel my balls pull up as my cock swells, and I still my fist inside her.

"Look at me, Ayla!" I growl, but her eyes never meet mine as I roar out my release.

I thrust into her over and over until finally I'm depleted. Pulling my fist from her first, I'm careful not to hurt her, but the moment it's free, I slap her clit.

"You were a very naughty girl! When I tell you to look at me, you look!" I chastise her.

However, I get no response—not even when I slap her clit again. Furrowing my brows, I pull out of her ass and walk around the table to check on her, and that's when I notice that she's unresponsive.

With a speed I never knew I had, I release Ayla from all the restraints, calling out her name and begging her to open her eyes. When I remove the gag, I'm horrified to see how much saliva she has built up in her mouth.

"Ayla—Baby—open your eyes!" I yell repeatedly, but nothing...

I check for a pulse, and that's when I lose my shit. The heart-wrenching roar that echoes through the room would be heard by everyone if there were anyone here other than us.

Picking Ayla's limp body up, I lay her on the floor and start CPR. I don't know what I'm doing, and the longer I do it, the more tears flow down my face.

"Please, Baby! Don't leave me—I've just found you. You're the other half of my soul! I can't live without you!"

One Mississippi, two Mississippi, three Mississippi, four Mississippi, five Mississippi, six Mississippi, seven Mississippi, eight Mississippi, nine Mississippi, ten Mississippi—blow.

Over and over I count, and then tilt her head back and blow, but I'm not getting anywhere. I've never fucking done this before! I've killed people, not brought them back to life! That's it—I'm being punished!

Sitting back on my heels, I look to the heavens and scream, "Take me, *motherfucker*! Don't take her! Punish me—I'm the one who doesn't deserve to be here!"

I try one last time to breathe life into the woman who will forever hold my heart, but then I collapse. I can't remember the last time I cried, but I do, and I do it for a long while.

I'm not sure how long I'm like this, but suddenly, I jump to my feet and move to one of the cabinets. I don't bother wiping the tears away; it no longer matters. Finding what I was searching for, I remove the blade from its sheath and go back to pick Ayla up off the floor and carry her back to our room.

Very carefully, I lay her on the bed before lying down beside her. "I cannot live this life without you, little imp. If you can no longer be here with me in this life, then I'll join you in the afterlife."

I'm quick as I glide the blade along the veins in both my wrists, ensuring that I don't get it wrong. I'm already numb from my loss and the fact that it's all my fault, so I don't feel the pain I'm inflicting on myself. Not that I don't deserve it. As an experienced Dom, I should have been more vigilant. I don't deserve the title of Dom. I let my emotions and my selfish need distract me from the most crucial thing—Ayla's safety.

Once the job is done, and my blood flows from the slits in each wrist, I pull Ayla into my arms. I brush the hair away from her face and gaze into blue eyes that no longer sparkle. Pressing my lips to hers, I close my eyes and take one last deep breath, inhaling her scent.

I remain this way, never moving, never letting go—not even when my heart stops beating.

ACKNOWLEDGMENTS

First and foremost, I want to thank my family. Putting up with my long hours and my frequent absences is not easy, but they take it in stride, knowing what my writing means to me. Thank you for loving me enough to put up with me while I'm in the 'zone.'

Next is my small PR team, comprised of my favorite smut ladies, led by my Head of PR and PAs, Stephanie K., Nicole, and their assistant, Kimi, who assists with my Hype Team. Thank you so much for all that you do for me. Also, to my Social Media Manager, Jessie, who is literally my saving grace when it comes to tech stuff. But above all, these ladies, along with Brittany, Kindra, Kristen, Kristie, Natalie, Brandy, Dalia, Stephanie C., Trina, Ashley, Kyja, Amy, Rachel, and Darian...keep me somewhat sane... most of the time. I love all of you bunches.

I would also like to thank my Alpha, Beta, and ARC teams for taking the time to read this title and provide me with their honest feedback. They truly are an amazing bunch!

THE SINNER IN ME

MORE BY STACY ROSE

The Bully Series
My Bully's Love
Addicted To My Bully's Love
My Bully's Best Friend
Loving Them: Our Happily Ever After

The Choice Duet
Aria's Choice
Aria's Choice: Choosing Them

The Twisted Duet & Novella
Twisted Hunger
Twisted Lies: A Twisted Novella
Twisted Bonds

The Nyte's Hall Series
Unholy Gods: Reclaiming Her
Unholy Gods: Keeping Her
Unholy Gods: Shattering Her
Unholy Gods: Mastering Her (Coming Soon)
Unholy Gods: Taming Her (Coming Soon)

Untamed Duology
Her Untamed Beasts (part 1)

Standalones
Saints and Sinners
The Devil's Heir

THE SINNER IN ME